Francesco D'Adamo

Francesco was born in Milan where he lives and works. His parents were refugees from Istria, Croatia. A writer, journalist and teacher, his adult novels such as *Overdose*, 1992, explore the criminal underworld in the Italian *noir* style.

His first novel for young people, *Lupo Omega*, was published in 1999 and shortlisted for three literary prizes. This was followed by *Mille Pezzi al Giorno*, 2000; *Iqbal*, 2001; *Bazar*, 2002; *Johnny Il Seminatore* 2005; *Storia di Ouiah che era un Leopardo*, 2006 and *L'Astronave & Vil Coyote*, 2006.

Iqbal was first published in English in 2003 and received the New York Christopher Award for Adolescents and the Cento Prize in Italy. In 2004, Francesco won the International Reading Association Teachers' Choices Booklist Prize.

Siân Williams, translator

Siân Williams was a publisher for many years, first with Writers and Readers Publishing Cooperative and then Camden Press. She now works as a translator and promoter of literature in translation and is the organiser of The Children's Bookshow, an annual tour of writers of children's literature.

She has translated a novel and a play by Dacia Maraini, a biography of Natalia Ginzburg and a novel by Lalla Romano and is currently working on translations of a picture book and a novel. She received a Hawthornden Fellowship in 2007.

FRANCESCO D'ADAMO

MY BROTHER JOHNNY

translated by

Siân Williams

AURORA METRO PRESS

We gratefully acknowledge financial assistance from The Arts
Council of England and the support of The Italian Ministry of
Foreign Affairs.

First published in the UK in 2007 by Aurora Metro Publications
Ltd. info@aurorametro.com www.aurorametro.com
Copyright © 2007 Aurora Metro Publications Ltd.

Johnny Il seminatore Copyright © 2005 Francesco D'Adamo, first
published by RCS Libri S.p.A., Milan

I edizione Contrasti Fabbri Editori gennaio 2005
Eve of Destruction Lyrics by Philip Sloan Copyright © 1965
performed by Barry McGuire, released by RCA Victor, UK
Translation Copyright © 2007 Sian Williams
Cover Photos: acclaimimages.com © Verna Bice 2007 Image 0018-
0405-1619-0327 /Dreamstime.com © Costa 2007 Image ID:
1698351
Production: Gillian Wakeling
With thanks to: Lisa Zaffi, The Italian Institute, London , Judy
Heckstall-Smith, Aidan Jenkins, Tessa Crowley.
The right of Francesco D'Adamo to be identified as the author of
this work has been asserted by him in accordance with the
Copyright, Designs and Patents Act 1988.

ISBN 978 0-9551566-3-2 Printed by Ashford Colour Press, UK.

'Some stories need to be written, and deserve to be read all over the world. My Brother Johnny is one of these: a story that closes the distance between us and the wars that we sanction, or ignore, but for which we should recognise our responsibility. It explores its big theme through an accessible, domestic, family drama – it brings it home, in every sense. Succinct but powerful, this novella, with its magical denouement, is a kind of parable, with a lesson for us all.'

Nicolette Jones,
(children's books reviewer of The Sunday Times)

'A haunting, beautiful story, subtly written and seamlessly translated... I couldn't put it down... no sermonising, but full of truth.'

James Riordan, author,
(shortlisted for The Whitbread Children's Literature Award)

'... a strong anti-war statement, with a narrative firmly grounded in the reality of a small, foggy Italian town - a reality which makes the story's eerie ending still more haunting.'

Susan Price, author
(winner of The Guardian Children's Fiction Prize)

'A vibrant anti-war novel.'

L'Unità

'*My Brother Johnny* confirms Francesco D'Adamo as a passionately committed writer whose themes have moral and social impact.'

La Stampa

'Is it possible to talk to adolescents about the hypocrisy of people who justify armed intervention? This book shows us how, in the wry voice of the narrator Belinda, whose brother is a soldier who rebels.'

Liberation

CHAPTER ONE

When Johnny came back from his missions in the sky Over There, there was no one waiting for him at the station. He arrived on the last night-train and was the only passenger to get off before it moved on, creaking in the fog and darkness, to continue its journey through the emptiness of the plain.

Johnny crossed the shining tracks, his blue airman's bag over his shoulder, passed by the greasy windows of the office belonging to Old Zenya, the stationmaster (who at that time of night was always fast asleep in his swivel chair), slipped out of the exit that led into the avenue and headed for the village.

It was very foggy. A damp, white veil hung from the trees and hid everything – you couldn't see ten metres in front of you – and besides, it was Hallowe'en, so no one noticed him.

Marione from *The Big Bite* said, later on, that he'd thought he heard someone go by outside while he was preparing another lot of hamburgers for the grill; he was waiting for the Hallowe'en crowd to arrive. But he hadn't been paying attention: he was alone in the place right then with all the lights on –

like being in a grounded flying saucer – and he still had to go downstairs to bring up a couple of barrels of beer and sort out the counter and the snacks. *The Big Bite* was a good place to end an evening.

He didn't so much as see him, he said, as hear the clicking of hobnailed boots on the wet tarmac; he glimpsed a sort of shadow, walking slowly, dragging its feet. He didn't imagine it was Johnny, otherwise he'd have woken up the entire village even if it meant closing the bar and losing out on business. He'd do that for Johnny, and much more.

So Johnny was able to slip along the deserted streets, avoid the piazza, skirt the terraced houses where big carved pumpkins lit with candles shone in the gardens, and finally get home without being seen. Not even the dogs barked as he went by, as if he were a ghost.

He opened the door with his keys, went straight up to the first floor, making the wooden stairs creak, and shut himself in his room.

Mum was lying down at that point, waiting for me to come home, flattened by the headache that drives her mad and her first tranquilliser of the evening. Dad was in the living-room watching the war repeats on cable that filled the room with a greenish light and the red trails of tracer bullets. He'd turned down the sound so as not to disturb Mum, so he heard the noise in the hall. He went in his slippers and pyjama bottoms, to see what it was, made out the large shape in blue uniform at the top of the stairs and called out twice, "Johnny, Johnny," in a hesitant voice, but Johnny didn't answer.

Johnny didn't answer for the next 36 hours either, nor move from his room, and even when you put your ear to the door you couldn't hear anything except the bedsprings squeaking every now and then.

While Johnny was on his way home, I was in the *Biberon*, a stupid disco decked out like a cross between a chocolate box and the spaceship in *Alien*, stuck somewhere in the fog among muck-covered fields and frost-blackened stubble, shoe factories and those Sunday hypermarkets you enter in the morning and don't emerge from until evening. Then you wonder how you've spent the day and what you did but you know that if you hurry up you can still catch *90 Minutes*.

I was in the *Biberon* with a *Guinness* in front of me (I knew if I wanted to I could have another one), dressed up as a ghost with the customary pumpkin on the round table at the edge of the dance floor. A DJ who was off his head mixed techno and Gigi d'Alessio, while The Best Young People from the village were grooving madly all around me.

I wasn't enjoying myself at all.

I was thinking: *I'll bite the first person who asks me to dance.* And then I thought: *What am I doing here, for God's sake?*

OK, two stupid questions, because I already knew the answers.

One: the likelihood of someone asking a fourteen year old (thirteen and seven months to be exact) to dance, one with very little in front or behind and a bit of a punk, was zero point something per cent so there wasn't much to bite. Also, though you're not allowed to say it, I am Johnny's sister, after all. Since Johnny went off to war my credit-rating had rocketed. Otherwise the Older Kids would never have invited me to the Fabulous Hallowe'en Ball.

Two: I was here after months of all-out war with M and D, stuff that made the American War of Independence look like a joke.

No, Mum, I won't be late. No, I won't drink alcohol.

No, I won't let anyone touch me (I'm actually afraid nobody will – see above).

Months. In the end I won and now I was here: my first night in a disco, my first beer, etc etc. Only to discover I didn't like beer and I was totally bored.

I'm complicated, I know. I'm a stupid mess.

Just like when Liga sings, *"There's some nights you can't stay here alone . . ."* so you get in a car with some idiots and sail the sea of Great Nothingness, in and out of the fog – there's always fog here – and hope that at the next crossroads you don't bump into another guy, like the one driving the car you're in, who doesn't bother to slow down and see what's coming. And then, when you finally get to wherever, it's exactly the same as the place you've just left so it wasn't worth the bother.

Then when I get home Mum will be awake crying – Mum often cries, to tell you the truth – and she'll tell me, "I was so worried", and then she'll say, "Did you have a good time?"

So what should I say to her – no?

She wouldn't understand. Anyway, I don't really understand it myself. Liga probably knows how to handle things better. He's sound, Liga, I like him.

Because I'm absolutely certain he'll come one day. He'll park his car in the piazza and, with everybody watching, he'll walk through the arcades, loping along like a cowboy with his guitar bumping against his back, then he'll stop in front of me while I'm eating an ice cream and even if he doesn't carry me off – what happens next is a bit of a blur – at least he'll answer my questions because he knows about the World. Because here in this village, no one knows the answers and, as far as I can see, no one even asks the questions.

That's why I was in the *Biberon* the night Johnny came back, because I couldn't be on my own on Hallowe'en or Valentine's Day or Any Other Day. And that's why I was sitting at a beer-stained table dressed as a ghost, wanting to get out fast and find someone who'd give me a lift home, which was pretty unlikely. That's why there was no danger of anyone asking me to dance.

I know what they say about me in the village: Belinda's strange; she's weird; she's not like other girls; she wears awful clothes; she's got a pin in her nose; she's got hair like the Last of the Mohicans; she's dyed it green; she's always in dirty baggy jumpers; Belinda's stuck up and thinks she's God's gift; Belinda will give her poor parents a heart attack . . .

Maybe they're right.

Air. I go out and smoke a cigarette. Before I go home I'll have to suck a packet of mints – that's all I need, to have Mum smell beer and cigarettes on my breath.

It's cold, you can't see the sky, you can't see a thing, only white everywhere. Johnny's out there somewhere. There's no fog where they sent him, the sky's always clear, cold and clean, full of stars. That's what he wrote to us.

Please let Johnny come home safe and sound.

Everyone here says Johnny's a hero but I don't want a hero for a brother, I want a brother who's alive. Johnny's fighting a war, and no one seems to understand that. According to everybody here, war's something you watch on TV. In *Bar Grande* in the piazza they spend their evenings watching the war and saying how great it is, better than *PlayStation*. The whole village is bathed in a green glow at supper-time, and the only sounds you'll hear are bombs whistling and the rattle of anti-aircraft guns.

If you look through the window they're all sitting at the table passing one another the salt, and there are these blurry shapes on the screen – the targets – in the square of the viewfinder.

Then you see dust rising from an explosion in a huge mushroom cloud and the target's disappeared, and they move on to the next.

"Don't worry," Johnny wrote. "There's no danger."

How can a war not be dangerous?

You get to see soldiers too, every now and again. Ours I mean. They look happy, not worried at all. They're not dirty or wounded or mangled. It's not like in war films. Not yet, anyway.

"What's happening there," says Dad, "is different."

How is one war different from another?

Perhaps I should ask Liga. I wonder what he thinks about it.

"They might even show us Johnny one day," Dad says happily.

When they finally took me home, I could see from a long way off that all the lights were on. Usually, there's just the light in the kitchen where Mum's bound to be waiting up for me, counting the minutes on the big clock with the *Fernet* ad.

They were both still up and they were so upset they didn't even ask why I was a quarter of an hour late.

"Johnny's here," Dad murmured.

I rushed upstairs, knocked and called out, but Johnny wouldn't answer or open the door to me. I stayed a long time in front of that closed door then tried lightly scratching on the wood like I used to when I was little and wanted a cuddle from my big brother. He used to call me "dumpling" back then because apparently for a very short time I was chubby and not stick-thin like I am now.

I went to my room and lay down on the bed without even undressing.

"Johnny," I whispered, "what's going on?"

At some point in the night I woke up. I felt cold and strange. There was a message on my computer. It was from Magda.

"Johnny's home, right?"

"Yes," I replied. "How do you know?"

"I know."

I had to believe her. Magda's a witch; everyone in the village says so. She feels things. And also she's been madly in love with Johnny since she was in nappies. Madly and hopelessly.

Magda was a year older than me and even thinner, if that's possible, with hair shaved even shorter than mine.

"Magda," I typed, "I'm frightened."

"Open the window," she typed back.

The fog had gone. The sky was clear, cold and clean, full of stars. And it was red.

I don't know how long I stayed there, curled up in front of the windowsill, with the cold biting my nose, looking out at the identical houses and streets, a drunken car speeding through the night and that awful weird sky. I didn't know what to think, and it was no use asking Magda for explanations. She wouldn't have given me any.

But I was sure about one thing. Johnny's unexpected return meant something: it was like an omen and it was better not to mention that sky to anyone. Not even to Mum and Dad.

They wouldn't have believed me.

Adults sometimes don't understand a thing, you know.

CHAPTER TWO

Next morning the sky was back to normal, grey and threatening snow.

Johnny was still shut up in his room. I tried the secret signal again, but he didn't reply this time either. I knew he wasn't sleeping. I guessed he was sitting looking out of the window on his ergonomic Swedish chair – a weird contraption he'd been mad about when he was at school. According to him it kept your spine straight.

"Johnny," I whispered. "Johnny, answer, for heaven's sake!"

At breakfast Mum was putting on her The Situation Is Perfectly Under Control face.

"Don't disturb your brother," she ordered, "he's very tired and he needs to rest."

Then she looked at me and couldn't hold back a miserable little sigh.

OK, Mum, I know.

I don't exactly match up to your idea of a perfect daughter.

I don't wear nice fashionable clothes. I don't use perfume with exotic names. I don't have little crushes on my mates (someone please explain to me what a little crush is!). I don't have posters of TV stars in my room. I kill at least two hours a day with Heavy Metal ("That's why you're always irritable, precious"). I've got a terrible personality. I'm often bad-tempered. I swear now and then.

Apart from that, everything's fine.

I listen when you talk to your friends on the phone and you say in that resigned voice of yours, "Belinda's going through a difficult phase, you know, rebellious. We have to be patient . . . "

Just think how patient I am. I've been going through a difficult phase for thirteen years and seven months and the next thirteen don't look like they're going to be any better.

And don't say it's your fault, or Dad's. Honestly. If it's anybody's . . . fault . . .

I dunno . . . It's got to be someone's.

Sometimes I want to disappear. I could be the Invisible Girl. In the meantime, I'll put on a jumper three sizes too big so no one can see me.

That way at least they won't look at me *like that* on the street. They won't crack jokes. They won't giggle. They won't all call out together: "Belinda, Belinda . . . "

I already have to put up with this stupid name.

I know other people like all that stuff, and they go all red and self-conscious. I don't, OK? There's a whole load of things I don't like.

Being continually compared to Johnny for example.

Johnny's always been Number One. The best-looking boy in the village, with everyone swooning over him. The best guy at school. Captain of the football team. Captain of the basketball team. Captain of everything. Responsible. Trustworthy. Sound. The Son everybody would like to have. Johnny the Airman, daring Sky Rider. Johnny the Hero, defending our Liberty and fighting for us Over There as well. A Shining Example.

Capital letters are always wasted on Johnny.

But if anyone deserves them, he does.

Don't get me wrong, Mum.

I'm not jealous of Johnny. I love my big brother to bits. I'd take the pin out of my nose for him.

Johnny's different from me, but he's the only one who understands me. When we used to share a room, it didn't bother him that I didn't change my gym shoes for months. And that time last year I ran away one night to go to a *Metallica* Concert in Milan, he came and looked for me on the road where I was hitching. He put me in the car, gave me two hard slaps on my backside which still stings and said: "One word and I'll give you two more". Then he took me back home – but he never mentioned it.

Johnny never tells tales.

Then the next day he asked me: "What the hell did you think you were doing?"

"Mind your own business," I told him.

"OK," he said.

And now it's Johnny who's in trouble. He wouldn't have come back like a thief in the night if he weren't in trouble. Maybe you don't understand him? I can't get to talk to him and you're here buttering toast while he . . .

"Johnny's on leave," said Dad. "I'm sure of it. He and the other lads have worked really hard Over There these last few months. And now he deserves a bit of a holiday."

"He would have let us know," I venture.

"He wouldn't have had time. You know how these things happen."

No, I don't know, Dad.

It's not like Johnny to behave like this, he's always been someone who writes and phones at every opportunity.

And don't say Over There. It's a place, a country. It should have a name, at least.

And don't say work, I beg you. What kind of work is it dropping bombs?

Johnny does it though, so that must mean it's all right. Perhaps.

I don't understand much about this war.

I know it frightens me and it seems horrendous and I don't want it to take my brother away. But it's not work. I don't know what ... But it's something else, I'm sure about that.

"Dad . . . " I tried to say.

"It's time you left, Belinda, or you'll be late."

"Watch out for the signs!" Magda had emailed me at 8 a.m., like saying good morning. There weren't any signs at school, only two hours of maths and a hissing

18

radiator. At 10 a.m. I finally managed to escape and meet Magda in the last cubicle of the girls' toilets.

We barricaded ourselves in, and Magda lit up one of those stinking cigarettes she rolls herself which leak tobacco everywhere.

Magda was dressed in black, as usual, with her round dark glasses and hair she hadn't combed for six days.

"He's in trouble," she said.

"I know."

We took two more drags.

"What's he doing?"

"Nothing. He's stayed shut up in his room since he came back. He doesn't even answer. Mum and Dad don't seem to notice. Perhaps they're right, and Johnny really is on holiday."

"No," said Magda. "I've felt for days that Johnny would be back. And you saw the sky too that night . . . "

"I don't know if it was real."

"It was real. Other things are going to happen in the next few days. Trouble. This is a horrible business, Lin. The war, people, everything. They act as if it has nothing to do with them. As if it's something distant, that doesn't affect them. But it's here too. You'll see."

I didn't always understand Magda.

Mum always said that she was a "one off", which means – if you get down to it – she didn't particularly like me going round with her. But she's the only person in the village I can talk to.

Subjects of conversation around here are a bit uninspiring: boys only talk about football; girls talk about boys and fashion.

It's a bit limited.

After a while you get bored and want something else. It's only a village, OK, I'm not saying anything bad, but sometimes I get the feeling we're on an abandoned sailing ship in a winter fog with a crew who don't know where they're going but keep on doing the same old things day in, day out.

I tried talking to Mum about it and she said, "It's your age, Belinda. It'll pass."

With Magda, though, I could talk about everything: we used to go off and hide out somewhere, far away from the morons, and spend whole afternoons chatting. Afterwards I didn't know what we'd talked about but I knew I felt better.

"Just the two of you, again?" my mates would say nastily, and then I'd hang out with them once or twice but it wasn't the same.

They were all nice enough people, I'm not saying they weren't, but I couldn't be myself and when I went home after spending a Sunday with them, I felt lonely and stupid.

And I cried a lot.

Magda and I only ever quarrelled about Johnny: she was convinced that Johnny was *hers*.

Just think! He's my Johnny, obviously.

In reality, as we knew only too well, Johnny wasn't mine or hers, he belonged to some twenty-something bimbo plastered with make-up and with blood-red nails. We hated them all without exception.

"Tonight," said Magda, "if Johnny doesn't come out, we'll go to him."

"Are you mad, how are we going to do that?"

"We'll find a way. God, Lin, he needs us, don't you see?"

"Yes, but . . . "

"Until then, keep quiet. They'll all be wanting to know what's going on."

"No one knows Johnny's here."

"So you say. You'll see."

As always, Magda the Oracle was right.

They began arriving during break, and then the whole morning, there was a steady stream. Mobiles were going off right, left and centre and the news flew about like wildfire: Johnny's back!

My friends from middle school came over, even people from the years above; several teachers came; some came down from the upper school on the second floor, even people who would never have normally condescended to come down to the lower floors and speak a single word to us Snotty Kids.

The crowd from *Bar Grande* came round straightaway, led by Max, who won a local championship in scrambling and always goes around in the leather jacket of his bike club and a cap signed by Valentino Rossi – or so he says.

When they came by, everyone drew back as a sign of respect: the crowd from *Bar Grande* are the ones who call the shots in the village.

They're the ones who decide what's in and what's out; who's OK and who isn't (better to be OK); who you've got to be a fan of; which bar you should go to on Saturday night; which girls are attractive and therefore worth paying attention to and which ones aren't (better to be attractive).

That they should put themselves out for a Nonentity Without Tits like me was unheard of, but Johnny was their idol and, either way, I was part of the family.

The time Johnny went off to rejoin his squadron, the whole village went with him to the station.

They got a band and majorettes to come from a nearby centre and the Mayor made a speech full of exclamation marks and long words. Everyone laughed and clapped: it seemed like a festival for some patron saint.

The *Bar Grande* crowd had even made a banner with the words:

JOHNNY
TAKE ONE OUT
FOR US TOO!

And they cheered as if they were at the stadium.

Why don't you go over there then, you bunch of chickens! I thought. This isn't a game of football, this is a war.

I looked at Mum. She was crying but she seemed happy. Dad tried not to let anyone see he was upset.

"You should be proud of your brother," he'd said the night before.

The only one who was very serious was Johnny – he said goodbye to everyone and boarded the train without even turning round. I'd hoped right up to the end he'd say something to me, something special just for me.

The evening before, when I'd gone to say goodbye to him in his room, he was already in bed.

"Johnny," I asked him, "why are you going there?"

"Because I have to, sis'," he replied.

"What do you mean, you have to?"

"I have to, that's all."

It wasn't a great explanation.

I'd looked at his blue uniform, newly ironed and folded over the chair, the bag with his things and the basketball with the signatures of everyone in his team that was presented to him after their win in the Student Championships.

Is that what it means to be grown-up? I'd thought. *To have to do things you don't like?*

Anyway, Max was now standing in front of me. I hated him.

He was a cheap and nasty bully.

Of course I knew he'd always been jealous of my brother, and while Johnny was away he'd gone around looking more full of himself than ever. Someone like him, he wasn't even fit to clean Johnny's boots.

Max looked at me with an expression of disgust. "They say your brother's back."

"Mmm."

"They say he's shot down loads Over There, and he's on leave as a reward."

"Mmm."

"Cool. Tell Johnny we're expecting him at the Bar, one night soon. We'll have a party so he can tell us all about it."

"Mmm."

He turned on his heel and left, followed by his gang.

I looked for Magda in the middle of the little crowd watching what was happening: she was furious.

Dad – !

Dad has a little shop in the centre of the village. He sells a bit of everything and everybody goes by his shop at least once a day. They have a chat. Dad's pretty easy-going and well respected by everyone.

Of course he couldn't resist the temptation to tell everyone proudly his Johnny was back. And news spreads fast here.

The morning was never-ending.

Perhaps Johnny had finally left his room and was talking to Mum. I couldn't wait to get home.

Magda sent me a consoling text.

"Come on. J always knows exactly what to do."

"Let's hope so," I texted under the desk.

"Belinda," the teacher called out to me. "What are you doing?"

CHAPTER THREE

There was no need for a night-time raid: while we were at supper, we heard the door on the first floor open and the stairs creak, then Johnny appeared in the kitchen doorway.

He'd taken off his uniform, was wearing jeans and a sweater, and had a long blond beard. His eyes were different somehow.

That's how, the moment I looked in his face for the first time since he'd come back, I understood that something really must have happened in the sky Over There and that Johnny had changed – forever – and that Magda the Oracle was right.

And I also knew, somehow, that they wouldn't forgive Johnny for it, whatever it was.

Johnny had always had amazing blue eyes – lucky him – two beacons which had driven the girls mad since primary school. Now they were grey and lifeless and looked like two dark holes.

He's not himself anymore, I thought, and my heart ached.

"Hi, Mum," he said. "Hi, Dad. Hey, Dumpling."

He sat down at the table, stiff as a board.

We all felt uncomfortable. We should have been jumping for joy, having a party but instead, no one moved. Dad played with the tablecloth.

"Johnny," he finally managed. "Well, what a surprise."

"Yes, Dad, I'm sorry I didn't warn you."

Silence. The kitchen clock ticked for a good minute.

"The important thing is you're well," said Mum.

"I'm well. Yes, now I'm well. It's over, Dad."

Dad didn't know where to put his hands.

"What's over, Johnny?"

"The war."

"But on TV they said . . . "

"It's over for me, Dad. I've left. I won't go back Over There. And I won't fly any more."

Dad opened his mouth and closed it again. Opened it.

"Johnny, you've always liked flying, it's always been your life . . . And we all thought . . . everybody here thought . . . "

"It's over," Johnny said again.

He got up and went back upstairs, still stiff as a board.

No one was hungry any more and no one knew what to say.

I left Mum and Dad staring at each other bleakly. As I went past Johnny's door, I scratched on it as usual, put my mouth to the crack and whispered: "I'm proud of you!"

That night a storm blew up which swept through

the whole village, dragging dead branches, roof tiles and posters through the streets. Even the houses groaned and in one semi down the road, an oleander was torn up by its roots, scattered flowers in the air and disappeared.

Then a huge storm burst with hailstones as big as nuts that poured down onto the roofs and machine-gunned the tarmac with a rattling noise, and all the alarms and the dogs went mad and howled till dawn.

The next morning there wouldn't be a trace. By now I knew that nobody would notice a thing.

Now, to be honest, I hadn't understood much about this war.

I mean, instinctively I'm against it and when they showed scenes of bombed-out houses and those poor people in the ruins crying and shouting, I'd say to myself: but why?

And then the women and children and those ramshackle lorries full of people with their pitiful bundles, Top Gun aiming at them, and those enemy soldiers with long beards, wearing slippers, and carrying the kind of guns you wouldn't see even at the siege of Fort Apache . . .

I mean, maybe this time the war's right and necessary. I mean . . .

And then people said that Peace, Freedom and Democracy were at stake . . .

I mean –

I know, I use too many "I means".

We didn't talk about it much at home.

Mum said to me: "There are so many horrible things in the world already, why do you need to think about that as well?"

Exactly.

Not that Mum isn't a sensitive person: watching TV she'd say: "Those poor creatures . . . "

But I don't know how to explain it very well, it's as if her world is limited to our house and the two metres of garden round it, to the kitchen, the dining-room, the twice weekly wash, looking after the plants on Saturdays and buying cakes on Sunday. Basically, it's as if the rest of the planet doesn't exist for her.

Well, OK, she has to take care of us and she's got stuff to do, I don't deny that.

At the end of the day she's the one who picks up the socks I leave balled-up every morning under the bed. Perhaps that's what it means to be grown up and I'll be just the same.

When you have the responsibility of a family, Belinda, then you'll understand a lot of things . . .

Dad looked at me with a disarming smile. "I'm against the war too, Belinda – who isn't? But if they've decided on it, it's probably right. Let's hope it'll soon be over."

At school, our teacher Mrs. Morandi showed us on a map where Over There was. It really was over there and it didn't look like a nice place to live.

Then she showed us a documentary film in the hall.

It was all confused and scratchy, because Mrs. Morandi, of course, doesn't know how to use the video and doesn't know that DVDs exist, but you could see enormous mountains which to me looked really beautiful and terrible and huge rivers and those valleys where no one's ever set foot, and stone houses, and all the sheep in the world, and wild horses and a whole heap of poverty.

At first glance it didn't look much like a place that could threaten World Freedom.

As we were swarming down the corridor for a break, Susy Wonderbra Alessi came out with:

"It's obvious they're savages really!"

I wasn't brave enough to answer back – she can't stand me anyway – and then, by and large, it seemed as if almost everyone agreed with her. Or anyway, the overwhelming opinion was: "Thank goodness we don't have to worry about all that stuff."

And that was the overwhelming opinion in the village too.

End of story.

During a boring afternoon when we should have been doing maths homework, Magda tried explaining it all to me.

Magda's an intellectual. She reads, she really does.

She went on and on for an hour with me nodding now and then, partly to make her happy, partly because it annoyed me to let her see I didn't understand a thing she was saying.

We'd thrown the French windows in the sitting-room wide open so we could smoke without setting off Mum's smoke alarms.

"It's an almighty load of crap," Magda concluded.

"Well," I grumbled, "I'd got there too without you going on and on about it."

"It's not that you're a bad case," the Witch lectured, "you're just hopeless. All hairdo and no brain."

"And what about Johnny?"

"What about Johnny?"

"Johnny couldn't have gone and done all those dreadful things!"

We thought about that.

"Johnny didn't choose to go," exclaimed Magda triumphantly. "They sent him there!"

"A soldier can't choose?"

"No, I don't think so."

"Sure?"

"No."

"Perhaps he could have said no."

"Perhaps."

Mum appeared at the garden gate, weighed down with bags from the supermarket. We rushed to the bathroom to clean our teeth.

OK. Now that Johnny seems to have decided to turn his back on the Crap, I wasn't too sure if everyone else would be so happy. And for once, Magda seemed to agree.

Johnny continued to stay at home, without giving any explanation.

Mum looked after him lovingly and – tactfully – avoided asking him questions.

Dad – tactfully – avoided asking him questions.

I was ready to flip and couldn't wait to ask him a million questions. But my big brother was avoiding me.

Friday evening, just before supper, there was a ring at the door.

It was one of those cold clean evenings in early winter.

All the lights were on in the village and it already had a vaguely Christmassy atmosphere: there was still a month and a half to go till Christmas, but nowadays preparations start earlier every year.

In the afternoon workers from the Council had begun putting up fairy lights (the usual reindeer kind of thing), the shops were getting out the fake snow, and in class people were talking about presents.

"I'd never have imagined Johnny would spend Christmas with us!" Mum said.

"The important thing is he's well," Dad said.

Johnny's not at all well, for chrissake!

Dad went to open the door and there on the doorstep was Max from *Bar Grande*, all dressed up for a party, with shiny boots and newly gelled hair. He seemed solemn and a bit shy.

"Oh, Max," Dad said. "What a nice surprise!"

"Yes, sir," Max replied, shuffling his feet in

embarrassment. "Good evening."

"Hi, Max!" Mum shouted, leaning out of the kitchen. "Come in, come on in!"

"Good evening, ma'am. No, missus. Thank you."

Then he looked in my direction, unsure if this was a situation where my existence could be acknowledged or not.

"Hi, Belinda," he mumbled.

I've never seen Max be so well-mannered.

"Well, Max, for heaven's sake," Dad encouraged him. "Don't just stand there saying nothing!"

"Yes, sir. You see, sir. We guys thought . . . well, not just us . . . that yes, in a word . . . tomorrow night at *Bar Grande* . . . There's a party for Johnny. Something like that. With beer. So Johnny can tell us everything, all the details. Everyone in the village says they want to hear him."

This was probably the longest and most complicated speech Max had made in his entire life. He was sweating from the effort.

"That's a wonderful idea," said Dad, "really a very nice thought. Johnny will be very pleased, I'm sure. How can I put it – well, you see – he needs a bit of company right now."

"Exactly, sir," agreed Max.

"*No, Dad*," I yelled inside my head, "*don't be so sure! Not about something like that!*"

I told him as much after Max had gone.

"Belinda," he reproached me, "they're his friends. These are people who love him."

"At least ask Johnny!"

Johnny appeared alongside us. He'd got into the habit of creeping silently about the house like a mouse, tall and muscular though he was.

"You did right, Dad," he said.

"Johnny," I begged, "you can't."

"I'm going."

"Linda," said Dad, "don't meddle in your brother's affairs."

OK. That made me laugh. The idea that I worried about Johnny. Johnny knew perfectly well how to look after himself.

But since he'd come back, he hadn't been the same person. And even if I didn't know what story he was going to tell them, I knew not everybody was going to like it.

I didn't need any more warning signs that night.

No hailstones, wind, thunder, lightning. I kept the window open until I grew numb with cold.

I felt guilty and stupid. Perhaps I was turning into an Oracle too, like Magda. Who was that person in ancient Greece?

Cassandra, that's the one. The prophetess of misfortune.

What did I know? At the end of the day Johnny might have quit because he was fed up and wanted a change of job . . .

Johnny has dreamed of flying since he was your age or even younger.

. . . maybe he'd suddenly started suffering from airsickness . . .

Come on . . .

. . . or from haemorrhoids, or . . .

Ugh!

or there was some other reason. Whatever.

Something happened Over There.

It was only a party among friends. Lots of chat, a bit of showing off. Rivers of beer. Slaps on the back. And maybe they'd even introduce him to some gorgeous bottle blonde.

You know how a uniform can be a turn-on.

"Rage rage rage" I typed to Magda.

And sadness.

The real truth is you can't stand this village. You don't like anyone. You don't fit in. And so quite rightly they think you're a stupid stuck-up girl with a bad smell under her nose. And these are all your problems, girl, don't blame anyone else.

I closed the window so I wouldn't die of exposure.

"Rage," replied Magda. "Keep it for when we need it."

Two Cassandras.

We didn't know it then but we were right.

We couldn't imagine what would happen next.

CHAPTER FOUR

That Saturday morning I got up when it was still practically night, and a pale band of light was just beginning to cut across the horizon out towards the country and the industrial warehouses. It was really quiet and in the distance a single lorry, its headlights on, raced towards the main road, the swish of its tyres barely audible on the tarmac.

I put on a woollen jumper and trousers, a tracksuit, All Star knee-length socks, pretty, fake Peruvian mittens (a present from an auntie last Christmas), Manu Chao ear muffs, sent a brief message to Magda (Come to the Vallone immediately), slipped downstairs and went out, being careful not to let the door slam.

The pavement was covered with frost, and you could see the large footprints Johnny had left when he'd gone running down the path to the station ten minutes ago.

Johnny loved to go running early in the morning and sometimes he'd even managed to drag his lazy, unwilling sister along with him.

I don't need to lose weight, I'm stick-thin.

You'll have a saggy bottom by the time you're fifteen if you don't get a bit of exercise.

Big loss.

But lately we hadn't done much of that.

Lately, we hadn't done much of a lot of things, to tell the truth, because Johnny was too grown up now to want to bother with a drag like me anymore, and anyway he'd been more away than at home the last few years.

Maybe I'd never realised how much I'd missed him.

A big brother is a pain in the neck, agreed, but useful – every now and then.

Johnny could make bullies who were bothering me disappear with one look; on Sundays he'd introduce me to older boys.

You never know, someone might want you. Problem solved.

Johnny dispensed Good Advice about Life to me:

When you're really in trouble, just scream and then start running.

Does it work?

Hardly ever.

Johnny pissed me off constantly with his Sense of Duty and Responsibility.

He'd always done it. If someone had to take two free throws one second from the end, it would be him behind the free throw line. That was why he'd agreed to go Over There, I think, because he thought it was one of his Responsibilities and he'd never send anyone else to risk their life instead of him.

Johnny was the Captain, no matter what.

I didn't need to follow his footprints to know where he was headed: he'd be in the Vallone, for sure.

The Vallone is a sort of enormous hole, four or five kilometres away, beyond the supermarket, towards the industrial area. There were still a few trees there and weedy undergrowth and, at the bottom of it, a large pool we called a pond.

No one ever goes there, so we'd chosen it as our den, Johnny, Magda, me and a few other people who every now and again felt like being alone for a couple of hours with the mosquitoes and a dozen slimy frogs croaking away.

From the bottom of the Vallone all you could see was a sliver of sky.

For the first kilometre I puffed and panted and swore, then after the station I got my second wind and began to enjoy the cold morning air and the wind on my face. Actually, I thought a little run every day might do me good.

At four kilometres I was sweating like a pig, I had cramp in my left calf and I was imagining what a horrible sight I must look to anyone passing. Luckily there was still no one around; Friday evenings here in the village people go on a binge, and Saturday mornings they sleep in late.

When I got to the Vallone, I slid down through the scrub, scratching myself a couple of times, and there was Johnny, sitting on a rust-coloured stone on the edge of the pond. He didn't even turn round when I rolled right into him.

"All right, Dumpling! I knew it was you."

"Hell, Johnny, you've given me a run."

He held out a bottle of water.

I drank and waited a bit.

"Johnny," I said after a while, "you can tell me about it."

"Yeah, it looks like I'll have to tell the others too."

"You don't have to tell the others."

"No, but I'll tell them all the same."

"Why?"

"Because they should know."

"And was it so awful?"

"Yes, it was awful. No, it was . . . humiliating."

Magda suddenly appeared between two bushes. No sign of sweat, naturally, and she hadn't tumbled down into the Vallone like me. She'd obviously read the message: you can never predict when Magda sleeps or when she doesn't, otherwise what kind of a witch would she be?

She came and sat down by us and immediately began rolling one of her stinking cigarettes.

"Good," said Johnny, " the Coven of Witches is complete."

I took an enormous drag on Magda's cigarette and Johnny didn't even tell me off.

He was really sad.

"Johnny," I asked after a bit, "what happened Over There?"

"When we arrived Over There," Johnny began, "it was late at night and we couldn't see a thing. The troop carrier, with all its metal plates vibrating, had begun its descent towards the runway, and it was only when we were a few metres from the ground that we could begin making out the lights in the allied forces camp. They were incredibly bright and powerful and I thought how clean and clear and transparent the air Over There must be compared with our own. This is stuff a pilot notices."

"Are the allied forces on our side?" I asked.

"Yes. We got out of the plane with the crew, stretched our cramped muscles and cracked a couple of jokes, then they took us to our quarters and assigned us our places in the prefabs, camp bed, duty roster, the usual things. I was tired from the journey and feeling confused and worried."

"Were you at all frightened, Johnny?"

"Well, it was my first mission. I was a long way from home, I was shattered, and when I threw myself down on the bed to try and sleep, I was convinced I'd never hear the alarm the next morning. But I thought about you all before I went to sleep."

"Did you think about me too?"

"Yes, Dumpling, you too. I fell into a deep sleep, I didn't dream – or at least, I don't remember dreaming – then something woke me up before dawn. It was the silence I think. It was a total, absolute silence like I've never experienced in my life. Not even a breath of wind. Nothing. I went outside barefoot, in a daze.

"The sun was rising, the darkness retreating behind me, and for the first time I saw Over There. It was a plain, all dust and stones, all burned up; a long, straight, empty road and right on the horizon, in the distance, the blurred shape of a cluster of houses. Later they told us it was a village with an unpronounceable name and that we couldn't go there. The people are hostile, they said.

"Then suddenly the sun rose, a huge lukewarm sun, and I saw the mountains rearing up around me on all sides. They were immense and very tall, all rock and ice. I thought: What it must be like flying over there!

"Did you do it, then?" Magda wanted to know.

"Oh yes, loads of times. It was very beautiful. Just think, I was flying, with the belly of my plane full of explosives, and I'd never felt so much peace in my whole life. Funny, eh?"

"Not really."

"Right. I stood there taking it all in while the camp was waking up. It was a proper camp, large, well organised, all fenced in and with little towers for the sentries. We didn't need anything. We had a bar, a cinema . . . "

"A cinema?"

"Not exactly first releases, but not bad . . . And the other guys were laid back, nice. We got on. We had a laugh and messed about. That was OK. Nothing to complain about there.

"But there was something else I want to tell you about: while I was there looking at the mountains and the sun and the plain I heard a sound. It was the first sound I'd heard Over There since I'd arrived, understand? Until that moment, it had just been silence. Even now, if I think about Over There, I think about the mountains and the silence.

"It was the sound of bells. Down that long, endless road, a flock of sheep were coming. Nice fat ones. And with them, two shepherds, very, very thin, bearded, dressed in those robes they wear there, with sticks in their hands to direct the flock. They didn't even turn to look at the camp and the runways, they passed by and disappeared, perhaps into that village we could just make out in the distance.

"In three months of missions Over There those were the first and only enemies I saw. And they didn't look particularly dangerous, to tell the truth."

Magda and I looked at each other and considered this information. We were thinking the same thing, but neither of us wanted to say it.

I finally dared to ask. "But Johnny . . . didn't you fight?"

"Oh yes. Twenty-eight missions in the first two months with my bomb squadron. The planes took off in a continuous flight cycle, from dawn to dusk, every day. When one squadron came back, another left.

"The runway was near the camp. Whether you were eating or having a little nap, shaving or writing home, you could always hear the whistle of planes taking off and smell the stink of burning fuel. You got used to it after a bit.

"'You show them, guys,' they'd tell us, 'we have to hammer them. Don't let up on them.' We hammered them.

"Almost every day I flew over those mountains and plains. I had my flight path, my maps and my co-ordinates. In fact, I never knew where I was Over There and I never knew where I was going to strike. It was just Over There, high up in the sky.

"I flew. I followed the flight path they'd traced out for me. And when I reached the point indicated by the co-ordinates, I pressed a button and released the missiles and the bombs.

"There was something down there, I suppose. An objective. An enemy camp. A barracks. A fort. A column of lorries. I didn't really know though. But if they told me to go up there and drop bombs, there had to be a reason for it, right?

"I flew high up, very high up. Below me I saw mountains and plains, mountains and plains. I've never seen places more beautiful. Every so often there was a cluster of houses, a blurry spot which could have been anything. I released the bombs, turned the plane round and went back to base. I made my report. 'Mission completed,' they said.

"I never encountered an enemy plane. Maybe they haven't got any. As far as I know, they never fired a shot from Over There. Perhaps some rifle shots. Can you believe it? Big deal.

"They might just as well have used catapults. No flying duels, no acrobatics. In the evening, after mess, we'd go to the Club. We'd drink a bit, read letters from home, have a chat. We'd tell one another what had happened. Nothing ever happened.

Don't let up on them.

"We didn't. One day, it was the third week of the bombings, one of our planes crashed. They never found out whether it had been shot down or what. It made a big impression on us, naturally.

"We knew those guys. We were all friends there. We looked at their empty bunks, the bag with their things, the photos of their girlfriends, and didn't know how to make sense of it. There was a ceremony too, very simple, very beautiful.

"I remember thinking it could've happened to me. Then I thought they were dead for no reason and I was ashamed that I'd thought such a thing. Poor guys, it wasn't fair on them. I didn't go out there to be a hero – you know that, Dumpling. And you too, little witch. It was my job, my duty.

"And then it seemed something you had to do, for everyone's sake. For the whole world, I mean. For Freedom. I do actually believe in those things. Well, there was nothing heroic about the things I did, believe me."

The three of us remained silent for a bit, listening to the frogs croaking. I'd stopped feeling clammy. In fact, I was beginning to feel the cold in my back. Magda moved closer to me.

"On TV they said . . . "

"I know, we watched it too."

"You watched TV?"

"Satellite, of course. Features, news, discussions, whatever you wanted. I looked at those images, listened to those words and asked myself: are they us? Did Mum and Dad believe it was actually like that, that what they were being shown was true? And did they believe it in the village?"

"Yes, they believed it, Johnny. How could . . . ? Everyone believed it. We believed it too. And they were always popping by the house, or Dad's shop, to hear the latest news about you. They wanted to know if you were well, how many battles you'd taken part in and how it was going and . . . well . . . You know, Top Gun . . . "

"Of course, Top Gun."

"And was that why you decided to leave, Johnny?" whispered Magda.

Johnny waited a moment before replying. He threw two stones into the water and silenced the frogs' chorus. He chased a cloud of mosquitoes away with a swipe.

"No," he said, "that wasn't why. War isn't something good, I knew that. Even if I thought . . . but I've got no right to complain, I knew. No, that wasn't why. It's because of what happened later, the last month.

"I'm not ashamed of those blind flights and those bombs I dropped on whatever. But what I did the last month Over There, I can't forgive myself for that. I don't even know how to tell you."

I remember thinking there was something deeply wrong in all this: Johnny, my big brother, my idol, hiding in a bed of reeds and pouring his heart out to two stupid little girls.

Johnny, I thought, what have you done?

CHAPTER FIVE

We waited for the sun to rise, but it didn't. In the Vallone, there was a sticky, humid mist thickening. I was cold and wanted to be home. I wanted to say to Johnny, let's leave right now, as if nothing had happened.

But I couldn't, I could see that too.

Johnny hadn't finished his story yet.

Magda took off her dark glasses for a moment, a rare event. I saw her eyes were shining.

"Johnny," I started to say, "for heaven's sake. Whatever you've done, you know . . . "

"Give it a rest, kid. Magda, roll me a cigarette."

Magda began to fiddle with the papers and tobacco. I'd never seen Johnny smoke. He lit something that looked like a coil to keep mosquitoes off and coughed. It did keep the mosquitoes away though.

"Last month," Johnny began again, "they assigned me another duty. They took me out of the Bomb Squadron 'For the time being,' they said, 'They've had enough. We're entering Phase Two.'

"They took me to the hangar. They assigned me a

slow, round little plane. 'This is your new plane,' they told me. I didn't like it. The plane carried ten thousand mines in its fat belly on each flight.

"Go for it, Johnny,' they told me, 'let's show them.' I showed them. Do you know what mines do?"

"Well," I guessed, "they explode, they kill."

Johnny shook his head. "Yes, they explode but they don't kill. They're not meant to kill. There are so many types of mine, they've done their research very carefully: there are some that if you tread on them they cut your legs off. There are some which . . .

"I left on my own, every morning, without the squadron. There was no need for them. The enemy resistance was finished, if it had ever existed.

"Phase Two. I didn't fly high in the sky any more. I flew low, with that fat little aeroplane, so low I could see everything, every detail: the fields, the mud and stone houses, the buffalo tied to the plough, the children who came out in the mornings and went to the well or the stream to fetch water, the women who came out to get wood. And maybe the same two shepherds I saw the day I arrived. There were so many of them with their sticks and their flocks and their slow way of doing things."

"I became a Sower. Every morning I left in my potbellied plane and did my Duty: I planted mines. I had precise orders: the mines were not to be sown randomly, but around the villages and houses, along the water courses and roads, and in the fields. All in order to create as much damage as possible. There are two million of them Over There, apparently.

Let's show them, Johnny.

"Oh, yes. I sowed. Those were my orders. It was war. Except that in war you fight with soldiers, but soldiers don't plough fields, don't go and fetch wood or water, don't go and play along the river bed. That's where women and children go. Where civilians go. Old people."

"Didn't you try and tell them, Johnny?"

"Yes, I tried to tell them. But it was no use. It was war. And we had to win at all costs. We had to annihilate them, terrorise them. When I got back in the evenings, after I'd run out of fuel, I didn't even want to go to the Club and talk to the others. I'd collapse on my bunk, think of you, and next morning it would start all over again. Johnny the Sower sowed tens of thousands of mines, and that's not much to be proud of. It wasn't particularly heroic."

"Then, inevitably, it happened. You remember the village we saw in the distance, outside the camp, where we were forbidden to go because the population was hostile? Well, we went there anyway.

"Not that there was much there, let's get that straight. No entertainment, no bar. But just the fact we'd escaped the camp and gone somewhere else seemed a big deal to us. It was a distraction from our boring days. Or maybe a way of not thinking.

"Anyway, every so often we'd take the jeep in the evenings and escape. There were a couple of, let's call them cafés, and we'd spend the evening there. The inhabitants didn't seem in the least hostile.

They seemed resigned more than anything else.

"One evening at the end of October I was there, sitting at a table in an open air café with a couple of fellow soldiers, under a dirty awning full of holes, on the main street of the village with its unpronounceable name, and I was drinking I don't remember what – tea, I guess, they only had tea.

"It was late, it was almost time to go back to camp. The village was in darkness, there were just some lamps here and there to light up the shadows and the white of the snow on the mountains all around.

"'Look over there!' one of my friends said to me.

"I looked into the distance. They were coming forward slowly, dressed in white, and they seemed like ghosts in the night. They seemed to be floating in the cold air of the approaching winter.

"I didn't understand at first. Then I saw them better: they were just children.

They were hobbling along that muddy road on their crutches, leaning on sticks and pieces of wood, supporting one another. I have no idea where they came from and where they went. Perhaps from nowhere.

"That night, in that unknown village, Over There, while that silent procession of ghosts filed past me, I understood they were the harvest of my sowing: the victims of the mines I scattered every day.

Let's show them, Johnny!

"OK. I'd shown them. And I had the results in front of me.

"What's the matter, Johnny,' my friends asked me, 'you feeling OK?'"

"I staggered up from the table, and somehow found my way back to camp. I didn't sleep that night: every minute I was waiting for those white ghosts to gather round my bunk and ask me why I'd done such a thing.

So Johnny, why did you do it. Eh?

"I wouldn't have known what to say.

"The next morning I went to Headquarters and handed in my resignation. 'You can't do this,' the Commander told me. 'If I can't, sir, it's too bad,' I replied.

"Two days later I left to come home. From high up, I saw those mountains and valleys Over There for the last time. And I saw those innocent, crippled ghosts again everywhere."

"I'm still seeing them now and seriously, I don't know what to do."

"Johnny . . . " I tried to say.

"No, sis', leave it."

He got up, stubbed out his cigarette, climbed the slope and disappeared. For once that bigmouth Magda didn't know what to say.

Nor did I.

CHAPTER SIX

I went home feeling really miserable. I had a big hot drink because I'd caught a cold in that hell hole. My legs were aching from the morning run and my head felt scrambled. It was the worst weekend.

I carefully avoided Mum to get out of the sacred ritual of the Saturday morning clean-up. I've never liked housework much. Actually, not at all.

I sneaked off with Magda and a jumbo box of tissues and we spent the day hanging around the village, not really wanting to talk to each other, much less to anyone else.

Even the weather didn't help: a dreary sky, a bit of mist, cold. A runny nose – and you just try having a cold with three piercings in your nostrils. It's not easy. No way.

Of course, in a village, everybody knows you and knows your business. Every two steps someone stopped us and asked about Johnny and about the reunion that evening at *Bar Grande*. The only place we could hide and be alone for a bit was the Vallone, but it wasn't a great idea to go back there and catch pneumonia.

What a life, exiled from my own home with a broom and a duster waiting for me, hassled on the streets by my fellow villagers' curiosity. I'm almost tempted to call the Samaritans. I wonder if they'd bother with teenagers who are sort of punk.

The real truth was I was suffering for Johnny.

They'd opened a new electrical shop recently on the High Street which was absolutely packed out at that moment: there were a couple of dozen new TVs in the window, that ultra flat screen kind, and they were all tuned to the afternoon news.

There were the usual images with the initials CNN on them: something that might be a target, or something else blurry at the bottom, squared off in a viewfinder; an explosion, another viewfinder; some bangs which sounded like anti-aircraft; the big hard face of a general explaining something, but luckily, there was no sound.

"What would happen," I asked Magda, "if pictures of those white ghosts hobbling about on crutches, like Johnny saw that night Over There, suddenly appeared on the screens?"

"They'd never let us see them," she said, "and anyway, it's easy for people to look away. The only ghosts allowed here are the ones at Hallowe'en."

True, I still had my pumpkin at home.

"It's just as well it's over for Johnny."

"Just as well."

We went and took refuge in Dad's shop.

Even in there it was crowded .

"Wonderful," he said as soon as we went in,

"you've come to help me." It was my destiny to be a slave everywhere.

In Dad's emporium there was a bit of everything: bed linen, things for the house, detergents, perfume. You could find almost anything amongst the great muddle of shelving and boxes.

"No one need worry when they come to me," Dad would say proudly. "I've got whatever they need, and if I haven't, I can get it for them."

I called it Ali Baba's cave when I was little, though it's a beautiful shop and not a bit like a cave. I'd played amongst those shelves for years and I knew where almost everything was.

In one hour I'd sold four pairs of red knickers – even if New Year's was still a long way off it's better to be prepared; various plunging bras which I would never – I repeat, never – wear in my life, even if I needed one; some rather gaudy costume jewellery; a toothbrush; a plunger for unblocking the sink.

Magda threw herself into the perfume department, making the stupidest comments to her customers – she kept saying charming, charming, as if she knew all about it, when actually she didn't know a thing. People disappeared, it got dark. We closed up.

"You talked to Johnny this morning, didn't you?" asked Dad.

I thought my dawn flight had gone unnoticed.

"Yes," I mumbled, "he . . . "

"Listen to me, Belinda, and you too, Magda,"

said Dad, taking off his glasses, as he always did when he was about to give you a Serious Talk. "Whatever Johnny did Over There, we know it wasn't his fault. He was obeying orders. And if he's decided not to do it anymore and resign, he's done the right thing. Now Johnny needs us, and we'll help and be near him no matter what happens. That's right, isn't it?"

"Of course!" we exclaimed in unison.

"Dad," I said next, "but now you . . . Johnny's talked to you too. I thought . . . "

"Johnny told me everything yesterday. But he didn't want to worry you and Mum."

My heart swelled. I hugged Dad.

"Persuade him not to go this evening," I whispered. "Magda and I both have this horrible feeling about it."

"Johnny's the one to decide," replied Dad, "and I'm sure they'll understand and support him. It's a difficult time for him."

"Let's hope so," I said, "let's hope so."

That Saturday night in *Bar Grande* there was the sort of crowd which comes on big occasions.

As Mrs. Morandi says when she wants to put it in big words: *Bar Grande* represents a microcosm of our small community. Translated into modern English: sooner or later everyone goes there. That night everybody was there.

There was Max, first of all, sprawling in the front row, his legs stretched out to show off his motorcycle boots ever so slightly encrusted with mud, his usual leather jacket, baseball cap and an arrogant look.

He had his court of admirers round him. Max adored going round with people who told him how wonderful and cool he was.

There were the Guys from the Bar, showing off coloured jackets worn especially for the occasion, with the names of American colleges on them, like in TV films. They were red in the face, sweaty and excited, making a racket and elbowing each other madly.

There was the Gang of It-girls as Magda called them, who were really girls from The Group. They wore shiny make-up, designer sweaters and loud lipstick, stuck their noses in the air, and looked just the right degree of bored.

The war Over There had as much meaning for them as the rings of Saturn – absolutely none. They were there because The Group had decided, and that was that. And Johnny was a good-looking guy, you never knew . . .

Here I am starting to be nasty. Tell the truth: you hate them because they make you feel like a floor rag. Have you seen how they look at you?

It's not true: I hate them because they're hateful. Full stop.

There was Marinoni, the owner of *Bar Grande*, who was considered a person of importance in the village because people said he had loads of money. He was in shirtsleeves behind the bar contentedly watching the crowd massing outside, under the arcades and in the square too.

He'd put up a kind of stage on a platform, which was used occasionally for some music group, with a microphone, tricolour rosettes and a banner:

WELCOME HOME JOHNNY!!!

"All at my own expense," he was telling everybody, "and the first round of drinks is on the house too. Free!"

Seated at two reserved tables, set slightly apart from the crush of the crowd, were some of the Moral Authorities of the village: Mr Lulli, first of all, the Omnipotent President of the Parents' Association since time began.

He was a dry, severe little man, and had the look of someone who's just swallowed a broom handle flavoured with lemon and almost as delicious. If you were late for school, if you behaved badly, if you answered back, or if you were dressed inappropriately, you could bet that sooner or later you'd be called into Mr Lulli's private office.

You'd leave the classroom with a heavy heart and a churning stomach, feeling stupid, ugly and inadequate, cross the grey corridors lit by cold, flickering, neon light, and get to the bare cubby-hole (hot in summer and cold in winter) where Mr Lulli would make you sit on an uncomfortable chair and first explain your Faults and then your Duties: Temperance, Obedience, Virtue, Modesty and whatever else. Mr Lulli could talk on for half an hour without ever changing his tone of voice.

At the end, I remember, his voice was like the dreadful monotonous drone of a trapped, angry wasp bouncing around the walls of that too small room. Sooner or later, it was going to sting you.

I'd close my eyes but when I reopened them the wasp would still be there, and out of the window behind the desk where Mr Lulli sat all I could see was the cold rain on the window pane. No way out. Then Mr Lulli would fall silent.

You'd fix desperately on any old spot on the worn, stained green lino and think: if I concentrate, if I keep looking down and if I manage to count up to 100, then it'll all be over.

I'd begin counting.

By the time you got to 56, you'd have to move – the urge was too strong – scrape the boots you'd forgotten to clean again that morning and which – admittedly – were a bit disgusting, or fiddle with your matted jumper, which was a bit disgusting too, or try and push your dirty hair out of your eyes, and finally, groan that you'd understood and that in future you'd apply yourself and do better.

"And that's what we all want from you," Mr Lulli would conclude, "that you *apply yourself*, Belinda."

I'd been to that poky hole two or three times and had always come out feeling sort of dirty. As I went back along the corridors to the classroom, I felt I needed to scratch myself madly, or run home and take a hot bath. But what I felt like doing most was something against Temperance, Obedience, etc etc.

Or even smashing everything up.

For God's sake, being fourteen is already bad enough. Just leave me alone!

But for Mr Lulli being twenty was a serious crime that only time, perhaps, could succeed in erasing. Being fourteen was unforgiveable.

He particularly loathed girls who were very different from the so-called It-girls, especially if they had a Mohican, rings in their nose and wore dirty jumpers.

Alongside him was his wife, the Lofty Patron of all the Charitable Associations possible and imaginable, swaddled in an unimaginable fur coat which had cost the lives, roughly speaking, of a million and a half little mink.

The lady was the Eye of the village, the one who established with absolute authority what was going Well and what was going Badly. She too, naturally, loathed girls who were very different from, etc etc.

I'd been forewarned, admittedly.

"They're hypocrites," Magda would say. She'd ended up in that poky hole on numerous occasions too, unfazed by it all, staring at Mr Lulli from behind her impenetrable dark glasses. It seems it was this which irritated him most.

Sitting with them was another pair of Moral Authorities who, thanks to Blood, Sweat and Tears, had made a fortune and ought to be an Example for all of us young people.

They were the ones who had little factories out in

the countryside, little hurriedly erected sheds, where people worked from dawn to dusk. Any time you went by, you'd hear the thump thump of the machines, sometimes even at night. The interesting thing is that almost no one from the village worked in those factories.

"Of necessity," said Magda, "they only take on Moroccans."

They said if we young people were good and applied ourselves –

. . . *what we all expect of you, Belinda, is that you apply yourself . . .*

– perhaps we could end up like them with beautiful cars and a villa with a swimming pool. There were some of those, just outside the village.

Well, yes, I wouldn't mind, but I'd also like to do something useful, worthwhile. Maybe a doctor, or . . .

I haven't really made up my mind . . . yet.

But there was something I didn't quite get in that story about people working from morning to night, and for pretty much nothing I'd guess, because when we saw them around the village, the Moroccans didn't look as if things were that great for them.

Meanwhile, that evening in *Bar Grande*, there weren't any Moroccans. They were the only ones missing, to tell the truth.

There was Mad Franz. I really didn't think he'd turn up. Despite the absolutely overflowing bar, he'd created three metres of empty space around him. He'd taken possession of a little table, dropped his 130 kilos of muscle, scrap iron, studs, chains and razored head onto a chair which had creaked ominously, he'd drained and then crushed six beer cans and planted another couple of packs alongside him for the rest of the evening.

No one dared look at him.

Mad Franz is mad, and no one's ever heard him speak: every now and then he 'borrows' a car and runs off, always at 150 kilometres an hour, never stopping, never taking his foot off the accelerator. Not that he's going anywhere: he's just going and that's enough.

The Police, the *Carabinieri*, the Traffic Police, the Motorway Police, they've all tried tailing Franz along the main roads and back roads over a 300 kilometre radius. Once they followed him for half a day, until his petrol ran out and the car stopped sideways on a country track, in the middle of corn stubble rustling in the wind.

Sometimes – rarely – they catch him and bring him back, but he nearly always comes back on his own, puts the car back where he found it, locks it up carefully and goes and sits in the piazza.

He was there and that was that. No one ever knew if he was thinking, or what.

Nothing matters to Mad Franz – they say he couldn't care less. Some people say he's an animal and it's best to let him be.

But there he was too, that evening in *Bar Grande*.

Maybe Franz, given the way he was, had never been summoned to Mr Lulli's cubby-hole.

Or perhaps he'd been there too many times.

Anyway, at half-past nine, after a supper in silence, we made our way with Johnny to *Bar Grande*.

A moment before going in, I remember I'd turned and looked at the piazza. We've got a beautiful piazza here, with the church and the Town Hall and the arcades and a flowerbed a little to one side, with only one tree surviving all the years of building works. It's an ancient elm, they told me.

A bit crooked, a bit withered, but it's a tree and I like it. People used to say: let's meet in the piazza by the tree.

I'd just gone in when I saw Mrs Morandi with the other teachers, some of our neighbours and my schoolfriends. They were all standing up, clapping and shouting, and seemed perfectly happy.

Johnny passed through the middle of the ecstatic crowd and got up on the stage.

I sat down in my place (a reserved seat, obviously). My heart was beating extremely fast.

"You see?" I said to myself. "You see how silly you are? They're all perfectly happy and everything will be all right."

CHAPTER SEVEN

Marinoni, the owner of *Bar Grande*, was pleased to do the honours of introducing Johnny, seeing as the Mayor had been held up by important business.

He climbed onto the platform amidst cheers, in his dazzling white shirt, gave us a big smile, flashing all thirty-six teeth, took the microphone, improvised a little speech which drew two rounds of laughter and three lots of applause, talked vaguely about Honour, Glory and Liberty, hoped "our boys Over There might resolve the situation rapidly and return home . . . " and concluded with the inevitable:

"And here's our Johnny for you!!"

"All they need is the bimbos," commented Magda acidly.

"They're here as well, don't worry," I replied.

Johnny got up, took the microphone, looked around, went to say something and stopped.

He seemed calm but a bit sad, as if confiding in Dad and us had freed him from the weight oppressing him.

His eyes, though, were still the empty holes they'd been the day he'd arrived.

He hadn't changed: he was still wearing jeans and a sweater and had a long blond beard which people hadn't seen him with before.

Until that moment, in all the confusion, no one had taken much notice, but now he was standing on the stage under the spotlights there was a murmur of astonishment. Everybody remembered Johnny on the day he left, in his brand new uniform and stripes and his proud, lofty gaze. Everyone remembered Johnny as an open, warm guy, easy to talk to, who got on with everybody.

They were still expecting that, it's understandable.

They were expecting a real Winner, someone who'd endured a hundred battles, perhaps a bit of a show-off, like Tom Cruise in that film.

And – perhaps – nothing would have happened if only Johnny had begun to speak, if he'd just found the right words to break that first awkward moment.

But Johnny was silent,

. . . go on, Johnny, tell them . . .

twiddling the microphone in his hands as if it were a strange object

. . . Johnny, tell them, tell them right now . . .

and someone in the room began to think that it was all really a joke, that some funny little thing was happening, and started sniggering

. . . or at least tell them some sort of story and get it

over and done with . . .

When it seemed as if Johnny had finally decided to say something, at the exact moment I saw him open his mouth, I began to hear the Buzz behind my back.

I took no notice at first, even though it was completely silent in the bar as they waited for Johnny to speak but then the Buzz grew louder and began bouncing off the walls, even though the bar was actually very big – and it would sting, I was sure.

He turned his head abruptly, as if someone had slapped him, and Magda and Mum and Dad and the whole of *Bar Grande* turned their heads, and Mr Lulli drew himself up to his one metre sixty, straight as a ramrod, impeccable in his dark suit, moved his chair carefully aside, clasped his pale hands together, waited until all attention was on him and let loose the Buzz:

"Johnny," he said in his low, monotonous voice, "I've known you since you were a child. And I've always been very proud of you. Very. Johnny is a decent, well brought-up boy, I've always said that. A boy who knows how to respect the rules, who always knows how he should behave."

Mr Lulli turned his icy stare on the room.

"If only all our young people were the same. And now allow me to say, on behalf of everyone I'm sure, how happy I am to see you, and how proud we all are of what you've done Over There. Our community has always supported you over the past months, and has continually prayed for you and your safety. So let me ask a question, on behalf of everyone, I'm sure: why aren't you wearing your uniform, Johnny? Why aren't you standing in front of us in the uniform you've honoured, the uniform for which so many of our young men have shed blood and lost their lives?"

Mr Lulli remained standing, waiting for a reply. You could see he was barely managing to contain his indignation.

One's appearance, Mr Lulli always loved to say, is an indicator of what's inside. If everything's correct on the outside, then it'll be the same inside.

Johnny the Hero of the Country couldn't turn up without his uniform and stars.

Bingo, I thought, *here we go. The Buzz'll show him no mercy and in the end he'll sting him.*

I looked at Mum and Dad; they kept their eyes lowered.

"Thank you, Sir," said Johnny, "you're right. And I'd really like to thank you all for this evening. I know you've arranged it all because you love me. I'm grateful to you for it. (*Clapping.*) I've come here to say hello, to say thank you and to let you know I've left the Air Force. I won't go back Over There. That's why I'm not wearing my uniform."

(*Silence, murmuring, then more silence.*)

"And now," Johnny continued, "if you'd allow me to excuse myself, it's been a while since I've had any time with my family . . . "

(*Agitation in the room, growing noise.*)

The Buzz raised his arm imperiously, imposing silence.

"What does that mean, Johnny? You owe us an explanation. You have your Duty to fulfil Over There. On behalf of us as well – we've always been proud of what you've done, you and the other lads . . . "

"No, Sir," Johnny said. "I'm not proud of what I did Over There. There's nothing to be proud of."

"But how's that, Johnny?" Marinoni intervened unhappily. "You and the other lads fought . . . battles . . . aerial duels . . ."

"No battles," said Johnny, "no duels. You need to know what it's like. I never saw an enemy aircraft. No one ever fired a single shot at me. Anti-aircraft was practically non-existent. Nothing. I dropped tons of bombs flying so high there was only me and God Almighty up there . . ."

"Johnny, don't blaspheme!"

". . . and down there they couldn't even see us, let alone hear the sound of our engines.

"I believe that in two months of war we massacred some thousands of civilians and at least a million sheep. Besides, there's nothing else Over There."

"That's what you say," shouted someone at the back. "That's war. Too bad for them."

"Yes, too bad for them," said Johnny, "and too bad for us too. You don't know what it's like Over There. It's . . . there's only mountains and poverty, and kids in rags passing for uniforms with an old rifle in their hands being sent to get themselves killed. I don't think they even know why."

"They're fanatics!"

"They asked for it, Johnny."

I saw Mrs Morandi get up and give one of those looks I know only too well.

"Let Johnny speak, for heaven's sake! We all know him. If he says these things it must mean they're true. Let him speak."

"Thanks, Miss," said Johnny, as if he was still at school. "I . . . you ought to know. The last few weeks the fighter planes hardly ever flew. The bombers stayed on the runway in the sun. There was no need for them. We'd destroyed all of that miserable country. Not that there was much to destroy . . ."

A voice called out: "They've got weapons!"

"I tell you they've got nothing. There was no resistance. Our infantry advanced without conflict. Our air force didn't have any more targets to hit.

"And then they gave me a new job: they sent me to drop land mines. They told me to mine comprehensively every field of grain, every river, every pond, all the roads in each village. And I did it. I had to. It was part of my duties.

"And now they don't work the land in those villages, they can't draw water, and every child who sees something shining in the grass and goes and picks it up becomes a cripple. How can I be proud of that . . ."

That was it. I think anything could have happened then. Everyone in *Bar Grande* was listening to Johnny. Some found it hard, for sure, but they were listening to him. Even Marinoni's used car salesman's smile had vanished for an instant.

I think at that moment everybody in the room was willing to understand. They'd been told certain things, but now Johnny was telling them that none of it was true, and up till then they'd got it wrong. They were finding it hard, but they were trying. Almost all of them.

It would only have taken another minute.

Then it happened. I don't know why. Perhaps it would've happened anyway. Perhaps the signs the night before made it inevitable. Perhaps not, because Magda and I had probably imagined them anyway. Who believes in signs?

". . . It's not a soldier's duty to do those things," Johnny was saying.

The Buzz jumped to his feet as if he were on a spring. He was a little bit behind me, on the other side of the bar. I could see his face clearly. He was livid. His features were distorted with rage. And so were the other people's at his table.

No one had ever publicly challenged the Buzz's convictions and right from the start, he'd maintained that the war was right.

The Buzz, Mr Lulli, had never made the *effort to understand*.

"You," he hissed, and it was the first time I'd heard him change his tone of voice, "you defile the honour of all those soldiers fighting Over There right now. They haven't deserted, not them. They're still at their post. Doing their Duty. And you disgrace our dead. You've talked to us about your sheep! Our lads have died Over There. For shame! Did you know any of them?"

"Yes," whispered Johnny into the microphone. "I knew some of them."

"Shame!" howled the Patron, getting up and shaking out her fur.

"Shame!" shouted other people in the room.

A row broke out.

I saw Dad yell something at Mr Lulli. I saw Mum wiping her eyes. I heard Magda cursing everyone and everything.

Johnny didn't even try and defend himself. It was as if he'd had it.

He came down from the platform, slowly. He began moving towards the exit, walking quietly, head down, hands in his pockets. We tried to follow him, but we were stuck in the crowd and all the confusion. Everybody was shouting.

Max got up. Until then he'd stayed put, following what was happening with a look both astonished and amused, making comments to other members of his gang and every now and then pinching one of the It-girls. I don't think he'd understood much of what had been said, but he'd grasped the ending perfectly.

He got up, urged on by his mates. He went over to Johnny grinning widely, the leather of his boots squeaking on the shiny floor.

I tried to drag Dad away, but we were blocked by all the people getting up.

Get out of the way, for goodness' sake, get out of the way!

Max planted himself in front of Johnny and looked straight at him. Johnny stopped and a huge silence fell.

Dad managed to open up a passage in the sea of bodies and drag us through it.

Max looked around, to ensure that everyone's attention was focused on him. He adjusted his cap.

I told you he'd always been jealous of Johnny.

"Coward," he said in a loud clear voice, carefully pronouncing the word. "Big Man, you're a coward."

In the past, Max would never have had the courage to say such a thing. And it would have taken one look from Johnny to put him in his place. He wouldn't even have had to get his hands dirty.

But Johnny took it. He put his head down even more and moved towards the exit without breaking his stride. With difficulty, we managed to follow him.

CHAPTER EIGHT

It was Dad who found the writing.

I think there are very few things in his life which have made him feel worse. He felt even worse about it than we did. Because Dad, and his father before him, had been born and had grown up in the village, and he really thought of himself as a member of the community, as everyone's friend.

It was different for Johnny and me: our future would probably lie somewhere else. And Mum had come to the village after she got married, and, as she'd remind us every now and again, she had her roots elsewhere.

It was a bitter blow for Dad.

The next morning, Sunday, even the weather was horrible. The rain was falling in soft, icy sheets. The clouds were so low they got caught up in the television aerials.

We were all in the kitchen having breakfast, still in our pyjamas. Even though it was gone ten, the lights were still on, and maybe it was this that made all our faces a nasty shade of pink.

Mum had red eyes. Johnny didn't say a word. Dad tried to make a few stilted jokes, which hung in the air like the smell of coffee. No one was hungry, of course.

I was so depressed I helped Mum clear away and then she started on lunch, banging things about.

Dad went off to get dressed, saying he had a few things to do in the shop. I don't know what Johnny did.

I started pacing around – doing my caged lion routine. In other words, I'd wander around the sitting-room like an idiot, go up to my room, come down again and start all over again. Repeat fifty times in a row.

I heard Dad going out. I heard Dad calling Johnny in a strange voice. "Johnny, quick, come and see!"

I went out too, still in my charming lilac spotty pyjamas, not caring if anyone saw me. I stood there in the pouring rain getting my feet wet and stared.

It was ugly. It was the kind of insult which makes you feel dirty, like when you're in a crush and some cretin gropes your behind.

During the night someone had climbed over the front gate, which is only a metre high, so it wasn't difficult. They'd trampled Mum's flowerbeds – you could still see big muddy footprints – and they'd painted very large in wobbly letters on the front of our house:

TRAITOR

I remember thinking straight off: *I'm amazed Max knows how to write.*

Or maybe he'd entrusted the job to one of his hangers-on while he waited on his bike, sneering and exchanging jokes with a couple of the It-girls wriggling about on the seat behind him. Then they'd have taken off again, tyres screeching, laughing like madmen because they thought they'd been so daring.

"We can clean it off, " said Dad. "No problem."

The little hair he had left was sticking to his scalp and water was dripping off his glasses.

"No problem," he said again.

I've often thought back to what happened next and wondered, so many times I've lost count, whose fault it was.

But I haven't come up with a definitive answer. How could I?

I don't think it was Max's fault: Max was just an imbecile. And it wasn't even Mr Lulli's fault: he was an imbecile too, of a different kind. And it wasn't the Patron's fault or Marinoni's or any of the others who'd followed him that night in *Bar Grande*.

The culprit had to be the Black Air we were breathing in the village.

Because the Black Air was evil and everyone had to breathe it, even if they didn't want to. If you breathed it, you became stupid and wicked as well.

Magda and I had developed this theory during our long afternoons discussing it. It seemed the only possible explanation to us.

It was Black Air, for example, which made the boys run around like mad things in the snow on Saturday nights.

(*Why would anyone risk their neck in that crazy way? Because they'd breathed too much Black Air which had turned them stupid.*)

It was the Black Air that made people spend Sundays among the shelves of the hypermarket looking at stuff they didn't need; and only Black Air could explain the It-girls' existence. In my opinion, Black Air had been created in Mr Lulli's cubby-hole and from there it spread throughout the entire village; according to Magda, the constant thump thump of the machines out in the warehouses only made it worse.

We'd never managed to agree on that point. Anyway it must be Black Air that led people to believe war was something you could make a couple of jokes about in front of a big screen while you were waiting for the game to start.

I admit it wasn't great as theories go. But maybe Johnny thought the same as us, even if we'd never talked about it. I'm only telling you this to try and explain why he decided to take on the village.

Though in actual fact, he didn't really take it on. I don't think that's what he meant to do. Johnny decided to expose himself to Black Air, to say to it: "I'm here, OK, come and get me."

Johnny might have changed, OK, but he was still a Fighter.

He went off after a very depressing Sunday lunch.

We avoided turning on the television: we didn't need news from Over There where the war was still going on.

When he'd drunk his coffee, Johnny went up to his room. We heard various noises from upstairs, looked at one another questioningly, and then saw him come downstairs again.

He'd put on his uniform with his stars, and his shiny combat boots, and had all his equipment packed in two blue air force bags. He'd shaved off his beard.

He could have been the old Johnny, if it hadn't been for the eyes.

"No, Dad," he said, anticipating the question. "I don't know what they want from me. But it's me they want. In my uniform and stars. So OK, they can have me."

He hugged Mum, gave me a thumbs-up and left before any of us could say any more.

Johnny went off in the rain that Sunday, marching with long strides like a soldier past the little houses where everyone, still at the table, looked at him transfixed, their forks suspended in mid-air. Meeting only a couple of cyclists in waterproof capes on the way, he got to the piazza, headed straight for the flowerbed with the old elm and put down his bags.

Only a few people were around in *Bar Grande* and under the arcades. Those that were came out to look at him, still holding their glasses of liqueur.

Johnny opened one of his bags, laid out all the equipment carefully on the muddy grass, took out a hammer and pegs and rapidly erected his field tent made of camouflage material.

It took five minutes: he'd done it so many times in training camps. Then, using two aluminium uprights as supports, he stretched out a sheet of canvas as an awning to protect himself from the rain and, holding it tight, secured it to the trunk of the old elm with nylon cord.

Next he spread out a groundsheet in front of the tent, arranged his things neatly inside, looked around satisfied, sat down, took off his combat boots, tied their laces together and hung them from a high branch of the tree, where they remained swinging gently in the damp air.

Then he sat down cross-legged in front of his shelter, in his thick socks and a big waterproof cape, waiting for the Black Air.

Over the next couple of hours, practically the whole village walked through the piazza to see what was going on. Some people stopped under the arcades to look and comment, others pretended to be there by accident. Everyone wanted to know what on earth Johnny was doing and what on earth he was trying to prove.

Marinoni stood in front of his bar for a long time, got agitated, waved his arms about, harangued the little crowd and retreated inside.

Around four o'clock, driving on the wrong side

of the road, brakes screeching, Max turned up on his bike. Some girl, looking like a drowned rat, was on the seat behind him, but he took no notice of the downpour.

He got off, parked illegally, noted the little crowd, saw Johnny, looked around for an explanation, looked back at Johnny, closed his mouth which had dropped open, took the drowned rat and hurried into *Bar Grande*.

It went on like this all afternoon.

Johnny didn't move and didn't say a word. He stayed sitting with his legs crossed and waited.

Towards half past seven the Army Supply Corps arrived.

Magda and I crossed the square, aware of everyone's eyes on us. We were carrying an enormous picnic basket and a battery of pots and pans that clanked in the silence. We reached the flowerbed, took shelter under the canvas and put everything down on the ground.

Johnny pronounced his first words in hours: "Up and outside, you two."

"Nossir, Mum's sent you supper."

We took off our shoes, tied them together with their laces and went and hung them on another branch of the old elm. Magda took a packet out from under her jacket, unrolled a Peace flag and hung it up.

"I'm a military man!" said Johnny.

"You were. It doesn't make any difference anyway."

We tramped about on the wet grass, sheltered

under the canvas and laid the table.

I'd brought everything I could find in the house – an assortment of junk food and nice things Mum had made – so it was a big feast.

Johnny lit his gas lamp. I took the CD player and loudspeakers out of my rucksack, set them up and turned the volume to maximum.

"What's that stuff then?" asked Johnny with his mouth full.

"Liga. Eat."

It was a strange sight: the three of us eating by gaslight, in the dark, camped out near the old elm. Crowds of people were gathered under the arcades, and it was as if they were in a different world, blurred in the rain like fish in an aquarium.

Wow, was I enjoying myself!

"Black Air!" I exclaimed. "Come and do your worst!"

"What's this thing about Black Air?" asked Johnny.

I didn't have time to answer. My food got stuck in my throat.

Learn to keep your mouth shut, I thought.

I looked at Magda: she's naturally pale but she'd gone white as a sheet.

Someone was crossing the piazza, but it wasn't Black Air. It was Mad Franz.

He'd appeared like he usually did, without warning, and was coming towards us. His enormous unmistakeable bulk was silhouetted against the lights of the arcades. We didn't hear the sound of his footsteps – on account of Liga playing full blast – but

I seemed to feel the stones in the piazza shaking beneath us from the weight of his big boots.

"Johnny, what shall we do?" asked Magda.

I felt Johnny stiffen.

"Ready to run, you two!"

Franz crossed the piazza. He seemed to be taking forever.

At every step he grew bigger. He stopped in front of the tent. Seen from below, he seemed even taller and bigger and more threatening.

I turned off the CD player.

Silence.

There wasn't a sound from the aquarium under the arcades.

Franz dropped down beside us. He smelled bad. He threw a six-pack down on to the ground sheet.

"What the hell, Johnny," he said. "Let's have a beer."

CHAPTER NINE

I don't think I need bother to explain why my classmate Susy Wonderbra Alessi deserved her nickname and why all the boys in school called her that.

She was a year older than me and – shall we say – somewhat bigger. We didn't exactly have much in common. We couldn't stand each other actually.

Susy was too much of a snob even to be part of the It-girls' clique; she went after the older boys, the ones from high school; she'd often stay in the classroom at break to powder her little nose or arrange a bit of hair that was out of place; she'd eat one cracker a day and did two hours gym just to keep in shape.

I thought she was a complete airhead: according to her, I was really gross. Equal and quits.

Susy, naturally, was ve-ee-ry popular. My popularity rating, on the other hand, which had never been particularly high, seemed to crumble entirely after Johnny camped out in the piazza.

When I turned up at school on Monday morning, I experienced personally how Johnny's calm, silent presence in the piazza could provoke angry, violent reactions.

I don't know why my school friends behaved like they did.

You know exactly why they did it. You say Susy's a snob. And what about you, then? You've always thought they were a flock of sheep.

I tried to get along with them.

Well, perhaps they tried too and you didn't even notice.

But I'd hardly set foot in the school entrance, five minutes earlier than usual, in a great muddle of umbrellas, wet hair and boots, when I suddenly realised something was wrong.

Electricity.

If you'd touched something metal you'd have got a 20,000 volt shock. But it was something else that was giving me a sort of painful cramp in my stomach. A second ago, when I was going up the three slippery steps leading to the school entrance, an evil gust of wind trying to get down my neck, I'd heard the Buzz reverberate there in the entrance. Then it slid away down the corridor to the toilet block and the lockers.

And it wasn't because Mr Lulli was around: it was my school friends who were *buzzing*.

When I went in, the Buzz transformed itself first of all into innocent chattering, then, little by little, as I went in, shaking drops of water everywhere, it slowly died down to a stony silence.

I slunk into the corridor where the lockers were, passing between two flanks of silent girls who barely moved out of my way. I tried to nod to some of the ones I knew. I tried to act cool. I tried to hold my breath.

That was the Black Air. I knew it. It's air which makes people bad.

At the same time I tried to look around without catching anyone's eye.

Where the hell's Magda? Why's she never here when I need her?

A small group of girls from my class had gathered at the back, near the lockers.

They're old metal cupboards, grey and peeling, where we can put our things. Generations of students have covered them with stickers, graffiti, photos and various inscriptions.

Susy was there, of course. They'd already taken off their jackets, boots and so on and looked as if they were ready to go into the classroom, just as they did every other morning.

But they weren't smiling.

And they looked as though they were waiting for me.

Magda always does what she wants. Think about it! She comes to school when she wants and then she's amazed to have a permanent place reserved for her on the seats outside the Head's office. But couldn't she arrive on time this morning for once?

That wing of corridor is dark and isolated, a long way from the front porch, the offices and the places where the teachers usually go. The ideal place to lie low if you want to stay out of the classroom for a quarter of an hour or so, while Square Root, the maths teacher, is calling the register.

The adults, it's understood, almost never come here. It's a place for the last few drags on a cigarette and the last moans before the bell goes.

That morning I was desperately hoping that Augusto, the school caretaker, would come limping along, simply to check what was going on, or even that one of the secretaries might need the toilet.

Forget it, they've got their own private toilet.

"Hey, girls!" I said upbeat. " Hi, everybody."

Ice.

Susy Wonderbra was standing alongside her open locker plastered with photos of footballers and trendy pop stars.

My locker was next to hers. It just had photos of Liga, Gandhi and Che Guevara.

A great combination . . .

So I had to pass in front of her.

"Uh-oh!" said Susy. "Look who it is. The camper."

Ignore her.

I looked for the key to my locker and of course I couldn't find it.

It was as humid as a monsoon in there, I was totally soaked and still wearing those stupid wellies that Mum had made me put on.

"We were all worried you'd catch your death of cold out there in the piazza, sweetie. You really have some weird habits in your family."

I turned round, looked her in the face. My Mohican

rose five centimetres.

OK, Miss 36B, you asked for it.

"Leave my family alone!" I hissed.

The others came closer. Behind me were just two lockers and the wall.

Trapped.

"That friend of your brother's, he's sweet too. What's his name? Franz?"

Laughter.

"If you like, Susy, I'll introduce you. Even though I don't think he fancies trash like you."

"No, I don't want you to introduce me. You can keep your trampy friends. You and your brother. You've always been stuck up. You've always looked down on us. The Great Hero's sister. We've seen what a great hero your brother is. Everyone has. Well, now you're finished. Over. Do you know what we all think? It'd be better if you left the village, both of you."

All I can remember thinking is: *Why?*

And then I thought: *I'll show you.*

And then I wanted to cry and slap her, but I don't know if I did. Perhaps I should have done, perhaps not.

I know I went hurtling into the cupboard behind me before sliding to the floor. I heard the second bell ring far away and thought something silly, like:

I must get to class or the teacher'll be angry.

Then I saw the others shoving and pushing forward in the narrow corridor. I saw them open their rucksacks and take something out.

It's all mixed up.

I didn't defend myself, I didn't say a thing.

I didn't even try and get up.

They must have planned it, I know it didn't all happen by chance. It was clear from Susy's satisfied face, she'd organised the whole thing.

They came at me, hurling insults, chucking stuff at me, laughing and shouting, then they swarmed off along the dark corridor.

Oh, shit, it was the start of the lesson.

I stayed there leaning back against the damp wall.

All in all, nothing terrible had happened.

I was just covered in paper aeroplanes, and there were loads more of them on the ground. They were scattered all over the floor.

And they'd written on every one in felt-tip:

COWARD

A very sweet thought.

Magda found me half an hour later in the playground round the back, where the volleyball court was. I was crying and trying not to let my bottom get too damp from sitting on a dripping wet wall.

I was full of rage and disappointment.

I was disappointed in them but also disappointed with myself.

I don't know why I felt like that.

I tried to explain it to Magda.

"For God's sake," she said, "no way it's your fault! They're the bloody cowards."

She told me that it'd got out immediately and that Mrs Morandi had made a big scene in her class and that the ones who'd done it were now feeling guilty, except for Susy who was still looking extremely smug – and that steps would be taken.

I couldn't care less about any steps.

I couldn't care less about anything.

Magda couldn't do anything but go back to class; she had no choice. I climbed over the rusty old gate and left.

To hell with it.

I walked through the rain all morning and it didn't help my cold or my mood. I couldn't go to Johnny in the piazza, or home to Mum, or to Dad in the shop. They would have been alarmed and worried. They had enough troubles of their own.

Hands in pockets and hood up, I wandered around the back streets to avoid the piazza and meeting anyone I knew.

No one was about. There were just puddles, gleaming tarmac, walls all sodden and cracked.

It was a dump of a place to grow up in.

Even the shops looked like dark holes with pointlessly garish signs.

I stopped under a balcony to shelter from the downpour, and from the window of a house opposite a middle-aged woman in an apron watched me suspiciously.

OK, OK, I'm going.

At one point I found myself on the edge of the countryside. There was a mixture of rain, fog and filth, a tree or two, some building works, an abandoned field, a warehouse with things piled in a heap, old washing machines, fridges in bits, broken down cars, and the incessant thump thump from the sweatshops somewhere close by.

I thought about Johnny, in the rain too in his military tent, and how lonely and let down he must feel.

I didn't understand what he wanted to show people by acting the way he did.

Perhaps he didn't want to show them anything.

Perhaps he had no choice, if he wanted to defend me and Mum and Dad from what had happened on Saturday night.

But I'd understood a couple of things that morning, when my dear class-mates had demonstrated so clearly what they thought in that dark corner of the school.

One: there are people who if you tell them the truth – and Johnny did that in *Bar Grande* – feel as if you've made them take off their trousers and walk around in their underpants.

They feel insulted.

They prefer to hear lies.

Lies must be like trousers for them.

Two: Johnny's presence in the piazza was like a boil on the bum for them.

It was annoying. It hurt. It continued to remind them of the truth.

And boils get dealt with, one way or another.

I hadn't thought about that before.

I went home slowly, sneezing violently. Even the weather was against me.

It had to be my morning of Dazzling Insight.

You get one every now and again in your life.

While I was trudging through the rain, I suddenly understood two other things: that Johnny was in danger because neither Max nor Mr Lulli nor the Patron in the village would ever forgive him. They're not people who'll tolerate a boil in that particular spot.

The other thing I realised was that the next time Wonderbra came in range I'd slap her hard.

I got home, told Mamma I had a touch of flu, went to earth in my room, took off my soaking wet clothes, dried myself and slid under the duvet.

I was still burning up big time because of what had happened that morning.

But now I wasn't afraid of going back to school.

CHAPTER TEN

I understood everything over the next few days.

Meanwhile, the weather changed, the rain disappeared and an unseasonable, oddly warm sun appeared, which Magda and I immediately interpreted as an Auspicious Mark of Fate.

Johnny undid the tent flap over him and dried himself out.

He woke early in the mornings, shook out his sleeping bag to air it, swept the tent, crossed the piazza, went into *Bar Grande*, and asked Marinoni's permission to use the toilets to have a wash.

Marinoni didn't really want him in the bar – it was obvious – but he didn't have the courage to say no.

Johnny would drink a coffee, thank him and go back to his post.

He didn't move from there all week, and what with the water, wind and sun as well as the beard, he ended up looking vaguely like the elm alongside him.

Magda went on and on about how – if humanly possible – he was even handsomer and sexier that way (. . . *he looks more mature, you see* . . .).

Tuesday morning at school, in second period, Mrs Morandi gave a very interesting lesson on the Historical Evolution of the Concept of Tolerance, in which I fully participated, continually putting up my hand to ask intelligent questions (maybe not . . .).

During break I armed myself with a salami roll and a fizzy drink, went back to the classroom, located Wonderbra looking for non-existent blackheads on her satiny skin and nibbling on an apple core, and sat down opposite her. Then I ate the roll, scattering crumbs all over the desk, drained the can, and burped discreetly while eye-balling her the whole time.

Five memorable minutes.

Like the staring game, only better.

Mad Franz got into the habit of dropping in on Johnny every day between his joyrides. He'd arrive whenever, sit down, take out a pack of beers and hang out for a while drinking.

He wasn't great at conversation, that's true, but he grew to be a reassuring presence in his own way. Why he did it remained a mystery. He certainly never said.

Magda, who's nosy and a bit like a terrier, decided to investigate the hidden depths of Franz's soul: she sat next to him a couple of times, turned her dark glasses towards him, at first beat about the bush, and then began asking him a series of extremely complicated questions.

He listened to her very carefully, grunted,

drained another can of beer then crushed it on the ground.

Another question, another grunt, another can.

They went on like this for a while.

I hoped the two of them would fall irresistibly and foolishly in love, like in that soap on Thursday afternoons.

I imagined them, Mad Franz and Magda the Witch, hurtling at 100 kph towards their destiny on the highways of the world, followed by a police siren.

Unfortunately, it didn't happen and Magda continued to be mad about Johnny.

My Johnny, mind.

The village split down the middle and that was probably inevitable.

People go through the piazza at least five times a day. They have to. The piazza really is the centre of life here.

So Johnny's presence didn't go unnoticed.

Most thought he'd soon get fed up and that's how it would end. They got used to him being there and after a bit – I'm pretty sure – they didn't even notice him.

Some people actually helped him and got into the habit of stopping to talk for five minutes.

A woman nobody had ever seen before came every day and brought him books.

A pensioner would come by at dawn, tie his dog to the old elm and stay there for an hour in the dim light, talking about war – a different war – in a voice so low you could hardly catch it. As soon as the piazza began to get busy, he'd excuse himself, untie the dog, and go off.

"Please forgive me," he'd whisper. "I like being on my own."

I heard him talking one morning when I'd dropped by before school to say hello to Johnny. He was talking about an Over There – another one – which was neither exotic nor faraway, but near, where there were no rocky mountains, no snow and clear blue skies, but only rain and mud, and men from everywhere dying in it, who you couldn't tell apart.

"In the mud," he told us, "everyone's equal."

"You escaped," Johnny comforted him.

"No," he said in that thread of a voice. "No one escaped."

A man came over from the next village just to see Johnny. He had a neck so thick he couldn't button up his collar, and the sleeves of his jacket were too short. Timidly, hesitantly, he came up to Johnny, constantly looking over his shoulder as if afraid someone might see him. He stood there, not knowing where to put his big, clumsy hands.

"My son's in combat Over There," he said finally, "and he writes he's happy about what he's doing. I wish I could be happy for him. Everyone seems happy. God forgive me, but I'm very frightened and I can't talk to anyone about it."

One sunny afternoon Mrs Morandi came with a group of children from school; even two of my classmates were there.

She might have told me.

She had them sit in a circle on the grass which by then was dry, made them take off their shoes and hang them on the tree, and then she asked Johnny to tell them all about it.

So Johnny told them.

A television crew came from some-telly-station-or-other with a crazy reporter who brandished two microphones and tried to install cables and lights everywhere. Then he began explaining to Johnny what he could and couldn't mention.

Johnny got rid of him.

"You can't stop me doing my job as a reporter," snarled the guy.

Franz, who was there, made a trumpeting noise and the crew melted away.

And, as expected, the Black Air came.

It grew denser and thicker every day, you could almost feel it spreading out under the arcades and in the streets.

People probably thought that Johnny would give up. But Johnny, like the elm, would spend his whole life there if necessary.

And that got to them.

It got to all the people who'd decided not to go to Dad's shop anymore. And to the ones who still went there but only to make him understand, more or less explicitly, how inappropriate they considered Johnny's behaviour.

"It's not right," they'd say, " to bring all this into the piazza. It's disgraceful."

One evening Dad came home and he seemed older and more exhausted than usual.

He sat down in his armchair, took off his glasses, rubbed his eyes, and called:

"Belinda, could you come here, please?"

His voice was strange.

I joined him in the sitting room.

Oh Dad, I thought, *what's happening to you*?

"Belinda," he said to me, "do you know you could have had another name?"

Bingo, I thought, *this is the Great Confession. Now he'll explain to me I'm a foundling, like in trashy novels, and they found me in a basket and decided to adopt me. And my real parents are Princes of Royal Blood and when I come of age I'll be able to inherit my Kingdom. Maybe I'm the Tsarina of all the Russias.*

Not that I didn't like the idea. I'd have nominated Magda 'First Court Jester' and all the boys would fall at my feet.

Not bad.

"You see," said Dad, "when I was young, before I knew Mum . . . "

"Several millennia ago."

"Many years ago, of course. I'd finished secondary school and didn't really know what I wanted to do. Sometimes I thought I'd like to leave the village, go to university, see a bit of the world, I don't know . . . do things which seemed to me big and important then. It was as if everything was a bit cramped for me here. And I wasn't very happy, even if I couldn't explain why. Maybe you've never felt like this."

"Yes, I have."

"You have? Then there was my father, your grandfather, who was always telling me: you've got the shop, it's not a big thing, but . . . and you've got friends, you've got everything . . . True. But sometimes I'd get on my bike and go for long rides through the fields in the fog and I'd think: I can't take this. I'd half a mind to chuck it all in and go away. And I would have done, if only I'd had someone to share the adventure with. But it seemed to me that the things I was feeling, only I felt, and I thought: 'If I'm the only one feeling like this, then I must be wrong.' I don't know if you understand what I mean . . . "

Definitely Dad!

"Yeah a bit . . . "

"You know, there was a student at school whom I really couldn't stand, and I don't think he could stand me either. He was so . . . rigid, so sure the right thing was what everybody said. I was confused. I didn't really know what was right or wrong. Whereas he never had any doubts. He's come into my mind over the past few days, I haven't thought about him until now. Do you know what his name was? It was Lulli."

"As in Mr L . . . "

"Yes. Don't tell anyone, but even in primary school he seemed as though he'd swallowed a broom handle. And it looks like he still hasn't digested it."

Crikey! It seems as if I've underestimated the old man.

"Why did you tell me I might have had another name?"

"Because you see there was this singer . . . "

"A *singer*?"

"Wait. She wasn't just a singer. Back then I used to listen to her music a lot. She was . . . a Voice . . . it was like . . . Freedom. She was such a lot of things. It was like she was saying: you can all get lost and it won't bother me. It was like she was saying: I can live how I like and I don't have to justify myself to any of you. There was a war going on then in Vietnam. Have they told you about it in school?"

"I don't think so."

"Well. She and a great many other people said the war was an obscenity. That it should never have happened. That bombing poor innocent people with napalm was a crime."

"What's napalm?"

"It's stuff that burns. They were dropping loads of it all over Vietnam back then. They burned forests, villages. Janis Joplin – that's her name – she sang about that as well in her songs, and she sang about how good it is to be alive."

"And then?"

"And then, whenever I could, I'd listen to that music. It made me feel less alone and sad. One day, just imagine, there was a rumour that Janis was going to do a concert in Milan. I decided to go. But your grandfather, you know, was a bit strict about things like that. So I ran away . . ."

"What?"

"I ran away. I went and hitched on the main road. After I'd been trying for about half an hour, your grandfather and his friend picked me up and took me back home. Well, I was eighteen, nineteen at the time, but I still got a hiding, and perhaps your grandfather was right . . . You'd never do something like that, would you?"

"Me? Nooooo!"

"Then I decided that if I had a daughter I'd name her Janis, after her. And then you arrived."

"And you called me Belinda!"

"Mum liked it. And of course I did too. I didn't leave the village. I listened to my father. I probably did the right thing. Actually, I definitely did. I'm happy with what I've done. I'm a happy man and a lucky one. But you know, you change over the years. Sometimes too much. Would you like to listen to a record?"

"Well, if you like . . ."

I knew it: he went to the stereo, took out one of those records – LPs they called them, vinyl stuff from a century ago – and put it on.

Crackles. Scratches.

Oh boy.

Oh boy, oh boy.

What incredible stuff.

It was everything I'd always wanted to hear my whole life.

It was everything I'd been looking for in vain for thirteen years and seven months of my life, without ever finding it.

Now I'd found it.

I listened to Janis, I listened to her voice and I thought about Max, the Mr Lullis of this world, and all the others, and then I forgot about them all. Completely.

She was one of the Greats.

And I should have been named after her!

"Dad, why are you telling me this now?"

"Because I was in the shop today, and someone came in, wandered round the shelves a bit, bought something or other, and while he was paying he asked me: 'Is it true that that's *your son* over there?' Then he left, shaking his head.

"Well, that got me thinking I should never have given up on Janis and stopped listening to that music and I should just tell people like that to go to hell.

"And then I thought it's not too late to make up for it – Johnny needs me and I should stay close to him."

From that day on, Dad would close the shop then drop in on Johnny in the piazza and stay with him for an hour or so. He even once took off his shoes and hung them on the tree alongside Johnny's combat boots, and they spent the evening telling each other stories and laughing.

It was more difficult for Mum, of course.

Perhaps Mum had never listened to Janis's songs when she was young, or perhaps she'd forgotten them faster than Dad. Or maybe she needed the village's approval more than Dad and I did.

I don't know.

The point is I used to see her coming back from her usual rounds with her eyes looking redder and her face looking more and more strained each day. She never went into the piazza to see Johnny.

"Belinda," Dad told me, "Mum's close to Johnny even if she doesn't feel like going there."

OK, I understand. Actually, I don't, but it's OK anyway.

"Mum," I said to her one evening, "I know your friends feel sorry for you because you've already got a weird daughter who doesn't make the best of herself. And now you've got an ex-model son who's out there in the piazza with everybody staring at him, not understanding what he's trying to prove. But shit . . . "

"Don't say shit, Belinda!"

"Dammit. I know as soon as you leave a shop, everybody starts gossiping. And then you get stressed out. And you wish all of this'd never happened. But goddamit . . ."

"Belinda!"

"Bloody hell, Mum. Johnny suffered Over There, more than we can imagine. And I think he'll suffer even more. And I don't care what the hairdresser thinks, or the owner of the mini-market on the corner. One of these days I'll go over there and lay into them all . . ."

"Belinda!"

"Sorry, Mum."

It's difficult to talk to Mum, especially if you're not actually talking to her but are really in your room, in front of the mirror, in your knickers and vest and an orange Mohican.

Speaking objectively, not a pretty sight.

It's even more difficult if it's an evening in mid November, you've got the windows wide open and it's crazily, abnormally hot. Apparently it's only hot here.

There's a wall of impenetrable fog around the village cutting us off from the rest of the world. A lorry driver managed to get through on the main road, stopped in the village for a beer and said:

"It's crazy. I've never seen anything like this."

The rest of the world probably still exists. At least, the TV says so. It seems it hasn't been nuked or hit by a tsunami. Nor burned to a crisp yet by the hole in the ozone layer.

Ha bloody ha!.

Some plants in the garden are already trying to flower. Thousands of ants are on the march, crawling back and forth. They've started to come into the house.

I'm frightened.

How much longer can Johnny hold out?

What does he hope will happen?

What does he hope to gain?

Perhaps Mum's right. After all, she doesn't have strange ideas like me

. . . well, she does have to run a family . . .

and she has got a lot of common sense.

Maybe it'd be better if Johnny came home and calmed down a bit. It might be better if I cut off my Mohican, dressed like a normal girl and forced myself to like traditional Italian songs.

Perhaps it'd be better if I forgot about Over There. It'll end, won't it? They say it's already starting to.

And Johnny won't be able to forget it his whole life.

I try to get in touch with Magda, but her mobile's off. I send her an email but she doesn't reply.

I'm frightened, OK?

CHAPTER ELEVEN

Johnny remained at his post in the piazza for the whole of a slow, very miserable weekend.

We were all worried, but he seemed calm and determined. "Johnny," I kept asking, "you can't go on like this forever. What do you hope will happen?"

"I don't know, Dumpling. But something will happen. It doesn't really matter."

He was getting nicely tanned in that unseasonal sun, and his beard made him look like a strange Indian guru in camouflage gear and woollen socks.

By now, Magda and I were used to going twice a day across the piazza, pots and pans rattling, to take him something to eat, and we'd got very good at it.

"We've got the entrepreneurial spirit," said Magda. "We could start a catering business."

"What's that?"

"A kind of canteen. Only it makes more money."

But it wasn't fun anymore, not like in the early days in the piazza, sitting in the tent next to Johnny and pretending to be little campers.

It wasn't a game anymore, not that it ever had been.

The Black Air was getting worse, becoming thicker and denser and more impossible to breathe.

More and more people under the arcades were saying they wouldn't stand for it anymore. They should get rid of him. He was messing up the piazza.

It was rumoured that Mr Lulli and the Patron were collecting signatures for a petition to the mayor, asking him to have the Guardians of Law and Order intervene. It seemed a lot of people were signing even if very few would admit it.

They said the school's Parents' Association – the Distinguished Chair was Mr Lulli, obviously – had made a strong protest to the Chair about the harmful spectacle afforded their children. In addition, they were concerned about a Certain Teacher who ought to shut up and get on with her grammar, instead of getting involved. End of story.

Well, Mrs Morandi's got sharp nails, she won't be frightened off.

But it was impossible to breathe any more.

The Black Air was contagious, like measles. Only you couldn't tell, because you don't get red spots all over your face. And it gets more virulent on Sundays.

It's been proved statistically.

"I think it's because they get bored," Magda said, adjusting her glasses. "They get bored to death here."

We were in my room, sprawling about, in our socks, hair uncombed.

We'd listened to a bit of radio, a few CDs, some TV, whatever. We'd flicked through some stupid cartoon book, some stupid magazine, two pages of a stupid book.

We wanted rubbish.

I'd massacred an army of spots and blackheads and then given in when faced with the enemy's numerical supremacy.

Magda was looking at a hairy calf, saying: "Why should I bother to shave my legs when no one's going to notice?"

Total mindlessness.

"Pay attention!" Magda insisted. At times like this, she gets unbearable with her philosophising.

"On Sundays they have to enjoy themselves. Or at least be seen to be enjoying themselves. They all troop out to buy cakes. Then they go home for Sunday lunch . . ."

"You have Sunday lunch at your house as well."

"Yes, but I only eat carrots and spinach."

"Ugh . . ."

"Then," she continued, "they have a Sunday walk, except when there's fog – three hundred days in the year – and later on they hang about the piazza and so, if you want my opinion, they get madly bored and produce Black Air in shedloads. Then they breathe it in and swill it around until the evening, when there's the post-match discussion about the Championship."

"The ones who go out with boys on Sunday afternoons don't look as if they're that bored . . ."

"I knew it. Do you see how you are? Thick-headed and materialist. It's useless explaining things to you. Get ready to do your duty and go and make up with your friend Wonderbra. That's what you deserve."

"The fact is is we're two terrible old maids."

"You're a terrible old maid."

"True."

Now I've replaced Liga with Janis (I had to get a photo, by the way, and put it on my locker in school) I don't dream about him picking me up on his motorbike from under the arcades while I'm eating an ice cream.

I've betrayed him. Maybe I could still let him come and get me anyway. Better than nothing.

To be frank, Magda's theories about Black Air changed once a week on average, and the cause, depending on what was happening, could be the Football Championship; adults in general who never understand anything; boys in general who never understand a thing either; the TV (apart from MTV); school, from time to time, especially when the Head got hold of her and asked her why she'd been late the last sixteen times.

But there was some truth in Magda's weird theory about Sunday, boredom and Black Air: on Sundays you really did feel it more.

And that particular Sunday it weighed down on the piazza like lead, just like the sun which also seemed sick and out of place.

As usual, Max and his sidekicks were using *Bar Grande* as their second home – or perhaps it was their first. They went there about ten times a day.

It was a place to hang out and have fun, where you could talk too loudly, show off the latest designer shades, crack mildly dirty jokes, follow matches on satellite, occasionally parade your latest female conquest and boast endlessly about dozens of imaginary conquests until the bar closed.

It was all Black Air, in short.

And every time they went to the bar, they couldn't help but see Johnny sitting out there in the middle of the piazza.

And they couldn't bear to see it.

In the beginning, they'd been so surprised they didn't know what to do. Then they'd made jokes and laughed like lunatics. Now they were very angry.

Johnny didn't give in, he'd been there a week and maybe he was winding them up – OK, of course he was winding them up. And then who did he think he was anyway, big man, after the way he'd looked that evening when he'd publicly confessed to being a coward, a chicken?

Chickens should go off and hide, not hang around the piazza.

Max began getting mad around five that Sunday when he arrived at *Bar Grande* to assemble his gang and decide – without any rush – how to spend the evening.

Half the village was already there, with the heat for an excuse.

Max was wearing a pair of jeans very carefully

ripped above the left knee, and a dazzlingly white shirt with a high collar. He had his cap with the fake Valentino Rossi signature on back to front and his usual arrogant expression.

As always he parked his bike by a no-parking sign, said 'Hi' to his gang waiting at the back entrance, stared at Johnny under the usual tree and was about to go into *Bar Grande*. Then he stopped.

I don't know what got into him.

Perhaps something that had been seething inside him all week exploded. Perhaps he felt the need to reassert his authority over the rest of the group. Perhaps it was an excess of Black Air.

Max turned around and his face was evil.

He looked his mates in the face, one by one. There was Prince, his hair massacred with gel. There was Lambretta, a mechanic who felt highly honoured to be included in the *Bar Grande* crowd. There was Bachini, nicknamed Baco, who always wore a jacket and tie, because he made out he was a gentleman.

The It-girls weren't there yet; they'd come along later when the boys had decided where to go.

They all started sniggering.

Max took two steps forward in the direction of the piazza. He came out from under the arcades into the sun.

"Hey, chicken. Are you still crying about your sheep?"

Mad laughter.

Max took two more steps.

"It doesn't seem right that, chickens killing sheep."

Giggles.

Johnny didn't reply. He stayed right there, legs crossed, sheltering from the sun under the canvas, looking down at the ground.

I wasn't there at that point: I was in my room squeezing my spots and philosophising with Magda.

Dad was trying to cheer Mum up.

Mad Franz was giving a Highway patrol overtime as they burned up the road after him somewhere out on the plain. Sunday was a bad day for him too: he got anxious and needed to get away somewhere, anywhere, really badly.

Johnny was alone.

When they described it later, they said no one lifted a finger to help him, no one protested, no one shouted: "Stop that!" And it would have been enough, because Max and his crew weren't tigers. But at that moment they felt they had everyone's approval, or almost everyone's, and anyone who didn't agree had obviously lost their nerve.

Max jumped on his bike that was covered in stickers and caked with mud, kicked the starter pedal hard, revved the engine to max but didn't budge.

The engine screamed like an animal in pain.

It seemed alive, and maybe it was.

It was an ugly bike, evil, all skeleton and sharp muzzle. Its tyres with their deep treads scored the old stones of the piazza, and you could see that, like Max, it wanted to seek and destroy.

I'd always thought when I saw them go past that Max and his bike were one and the same, both of them tense, nervous, at odds with the whole world for their own mysterious reasons, and above all intent on showing them.

"Chicken," Max kept repeating, "chicken."

Prince and Baco climbed on their bikes too and lined up alongside their chief.

They had elegant bikes, like gentlemen. They stayed there motionless, one either side as if at the start of a race, and whenever they revved their engines, the roar bounced off the arcades and the buildings around the piazza. They were psyching themselves up, preparing for an attack like a pack of savage wolves.

"Go!!" yelled Max and, tyres screeching, his bike sprang forward, sniffing the air, followed by the other two.

They cut across the piazza diagonally, trailing sparks and smoke, aiming right at Johnny and his tent.

Maybe they didn't want to hurt him, maybe they only wanted to make him run, to humiliate him, so the whole village would know who really had guts. Or perhaps they were just blinded by hate, rage and Black Air.

They rode straight at him.

Johnny didn't move, so people told me.

He watched them coming at him insanely fast, their engines screaming and burning in the hot air of that November afternoon, and he didn't bat an eyelid.

A few metres from the tent, Max swerved sharply, just brushing it, went right back to the end of the piazza, braked, turned the bike, doing a wheelie, and stopped dead, waiting for the other two.

Then they set off again.

This time, a wheel cut one of the guy ropes and the tent collapsed.

From under the arcades, someone clapped.

"They were acting like Red Indians in the movies," Lambretta said later with an air of satisfaction. "You know, when they attacked the wagons. At every turn they made the circle tighter. Really tight."

And at every turn they became more evil. At every turn they got closer.

Johnny never moved.

"Chicken!" Max went on yelling. "Chicken!"

His face was red and swollen like his friends.

I don't know how it would've ended.

Perhaps they really would have hurt Johnny. Very badly. They were totally out of control at that point.

In the confusion, no one had noticed a cloud of dust on the horizon, rapidly approaching. The noise of the car was drowned by the motorbikes.

Max and his gang were still closing the circle around Johnny when a BMW with a smashed headlight and a crushed wing landed heavily in the piazza. Its windscreen was so covered in dust it was impossible to make out the driver.

It seemed like a ghost car, they told us.

It slewed to a stop and sat heavily in the sun, black and scratched from having gone through too many fields of stubble.

Max stopped. The other two stopped.

It was as if someone – finally – had broken the spell that everyone was under.

The people under the arcades shook themselves, started, woke up. Someone began walking away.

The party was over.

A door of the BMW opened slowly, squealing on hinges tested by the long ride.

Mad Franz had given the police the slip on the main road 30 kilometres to the south west, driving one-handed. He was in a terrible mood: it wasn't fun unless they really went for it. Must have been a right amateur following him.

He manoeuvred his great bulk out of the car, holding a can of warm beer in one hand and in the other a terrifying inner tube, two metres long, which must have weighed a ton.

I don't know where he'd got it, or why.

Maybe because somehow he knew more than us.

He shook it twice at Max and his mates, who vanished.

When someone finally told us what had happened and we all ran to the piazza, there was hardly anyone there. Everyone had gone home for supper.

Johnny and Franz were sitting on what remained of the tent. Someone had torn down the Peace flag and I wanted to cry. For the Peace flag. For Johnny, for everything.

"Johnny, come home," we begged.

Nothing doing.

He had Franz help him put the tent up again. He even asked Magda: "Bring me another flag."

We wanted to stay there with him.

"Franz's staying," he reassured us.

In fact, from that evening on, Franz didn't leave his side for a second.

"It's over," Magda murmured in my ear, as we went home, miserably.

"What's over?"

"Everything. It's about to happen."

"Shit. I'm already freaked out and you're talking in riddles."

"Something's about to happen, I know."

Sometimes I can't stand Magda. I was tired, depressed, fed up. Dad and Mum were as limp as two rags. Magda wasn't much help either.

But she was right, I knew that too.

Ghosts always come back, sooner or later.

CHAPTER TWELVE

Monday morning, we've got a test at school. Tuesday, too.

Why have you got it in for me then, tell me . . .

I spend afternoons at home listening to music on those old vinyl discs of Dad's. Especially to Janis. She sings about a boy who'll come and get her in a *Mercedes Benz* or about some *Bobby McGee*.

And then I tried translating an old song from the same period, *Eve of Destruction*, by someone called Barry McGuire, which in the original goes more or less (I've never been great at English):

The Eastern World it is explodin',
Violence flarin',
Blood flowin'
You're old enough to kill,
but not for votin':
You don't believe in war
But what's that gun you're totin'?
Don't you understand what I'm trying to say?
Can't you feel the fears I'm feeling today?

Stuff from forty years ago. I can't even begin to

imagine it. I have a profound thought: this good old world hasn't changed much since then.

Hours drag on.

Mum's holed up in the kitchen. Dad keeps putting the Back Soon sign in the window, goes to the piazza to see Johnny, comes back to the house, gets agitated, can't do a thing, goes back again.

The sun's suddenly disappeared, it's turned all grey and gloomy.

A strong biting wind's blown up.

"You should take Johnny another jumper," Mum says.

We try and pretend nothing's happening, as if it were just another day, but it's no good.

"*. . . Can't you feel the fears I'm feeling today?*"

Mum keeps trying to find me things to do: "Clean up your room, Belinda, it's a tip."

I'm almost grateful to her for once. Because while I'm busy, I can't think.

A tip is an exaggeration, though.

Yes, there's a bit of dust, and it's a bit untidy.

I arm myself with dusters, scrubbing brushes, and good intentions. There's a mountain of stuff to tidy, I'll never finish, but that's OK.

If Johnny stops being stubborn and comes home and nothing happens, I promise I'll clean my room every day. At least twice a week. OK, three times then.

There are manky socks all over the place. I'd really like to know who's having fun leaving these dirty socks in my room. It's disgraceful.

Memories of an entire life surface: tickets, notes,

photos cut out of magazines, various bits of home-work I'd hidden.

I slog away for two hours and, by the end, it's the same mess it was in the beginning.

I leaf through an old diary, one of those you can lock with a little padlock for privacy (luckily, the padlock's lost – I never would've been able to find the key) and happy to discover that two years ago I was almost as stupid as I am now.

I open the window.

There are ominous black clouds. It'll rain or snow tonight. They're low, the sky's leaden. In weather like this, the village is silent and still.

They're all at home, as if they're brooding about something.

I hear Dad come in again.

I go downstairs.

Mum's put on her good suit, combed her hair carefully. She's filled a thermos.

"I'm taking Johnny his supper," she says.

I'm about to say to her: "I'll come with you," but I realise it's better not to.

It'll be the first time Mum's gone to the piazza.

Perhaps she's seen those black clouds too, perhaps she's also heard that sort of rumbling noise that's been buzzing in my ears for the last few minutes: it's a dreary, indistinct, hollow sort of noise.

It's coming from above the clouds, and I don't know what it is.

It's just a storm coming.

That's not true.

Dad and I are left on our own, sitting in the kitchen. We don't talk. Dad picks at a bit of bread.

There's the tick tock of that stupid clock with the *Fernet* ad.

Mum comes back and we have supper.

"How's Johnny?"

"Fine."

The noise is getting louder. Very slowly, but it's growing. And the black clouds are now a solid compact mass, like a slab of slate covering the entire village.

"Can you hear it?" Magda texts.

"Yes," I reply.

No one wants to watch TV.

Mum goes to bed early. Dad flips through a book in his armchair.

I go up to my room.

There's an unbearable smell of cleaning.

I stand by the window looking at the iron-grey sky.

The wind's suddenly dropped.

The rumble's growing.

OK, I think, something's going to happen.

The mobile rings.

Magda.

"Turn on the TV, quickly."

I go into the sitting-room. There's a special news bulletin.

The war Over There has ended.

The enemy's surrendered.

They show long columns of barefoot men

marching with their hands up. Tanks patrol the streets of some city and people watch them from the pavement. Someone salutes. Our troops celebrate.

Comments: they are all ecstatically happy.

It all seems fake to me, like some film.

I'm not happy, I feel like crying.

That noise from the sky. It's loud now, and getting louder all the time.

"Dad," I say, "Mum. Johnny's in danger."

CHAPTER THIRTEEN

That Tuesday, the day the war ended Over There, the *Bar Grande* regulars met straightaway, right after supper. It wasn't going to be a good evening, that was obvious.

There was that weather for a start, with the slab of slate weighing down on the village.

The It-girls holed up at home. And, let's be honest, no one wanted them getting in the way. Better like that.

The anger they'd stirred up that Sunday afternoon.

"And that animal defending him!" Max kept repeating.

Every now and again, he'd get up, peep through the curtains at the two shadows camped out in the piazza, come back and sit down looking nervous.

"He needs a lesson from someone," he said again.

Bar Grande was almost deserted. Marinoni had turned off nearly all the lights, leaving only the ones round the counter, and he stood there, the little spotlights on him, a toothpick in his teeth and his supper turning to acid in his stomach.

He looked like the captain of a ship becalmed in the middle of a sea.

No one went by outside.

The boys had watched TV a bit, making comments loudly. Baco and Lambretta had had a long argument about something no one could make head or tail of.

Max had stopped getting up and down and had stayed seated with his feet resting on a table, fiddling about with his lighter. He didn't say a word but you could see he was going over and over some idea in his head.

At 10.30 they were on their fourth beer and had ordered another round.

At 10.50 the Special News Bulletin announced the end of the war Over There, Our Boys' Victory and the defeat of the Enemy, and it was that – I think – which set them off.

They were half drunk at that point and full of rage and Black Air.

They welcomed the news with loud shouts of joy. They hugged one another and gave high fives like at the Champions' League final. Then they'd looked at one another proudly, as if they'd won the war.

"Another round, lads," Marinoni had proposed. "It's on me."

They'd gathered round under the light from the bar counter, making a racket and slapping one another on the back.

"I propose a toast," Marinoni had said solemnly, "to our boys who have brought honour to themselves

Over There."

They raised their glasses.

"Yes," said Max, "to the ones who didn't run away."

And he turned to look towards the piazza.

Suddenly it began raining.

Without any warning, as if the steel-grey skies pressing down on the village had suddenly dissolved.

It was a thick, heavy rain, a blanket of water so dense you couldn't see three metres in front of you.

And it was black, I swear.

And silent. It came down noiselessly, not even a splish splash on the bodywork of the car.

The only sound – getting louder all the time – was that rumbling in the sky, but it was impossible to make out what it was.

Can you hear it, Dad, can you hear it too?

Dad switched on the windscreen wipers in vain, skidded, got back onto the carriageway, slowed down.

The piazza seemed very far away.

Hurry!

By now all the lights were on in the houses and you could see people looking through the windows up at the sky, marvelling at the rain.

. . . can they hear it too?

And that noise, growing and growing.

Magda flashed me a "Hurry, hurry" on my mobile. She was already at the piazza – she lives nearer.

Dad went the wrong way up the last stretch of

the Corso. I don't think he's ever done anything like that in his whole life.

Puddles. Two walls of water. Darkness.

The piazza.

We got out. An instant later I was soaked to the skin, black rain drenching my clothes, hair in my eyes.

Because of that, nobody moved. Not me, Dad or Mum. It was as if we were rooted to the spot, flattened by that wall of water and fear and shock.

There they were, but we could barely see them.

The tent had collapsed; it was now a soaking rag splattered across the stones of the piazza.

Johnny was sitting calmly in his usual place, legs crossed, hands resting on his knees, head bent. The wind raged around him.

He looked as if he were sleeping, or in a trance.

Mad Franz was standing alongside him, his shaven head shining in the darkness, rain streaming down his leather jacket.

He was holding the metal tubing in both hands and whirling it around like an Indian club against his attackers.

They'd surrounded him. There were seven of them.

Max, Prince, Baco, Lambretta and three others who must have joined them somewhere along the line.

Max had a chain. I don't know if he'd taken it off his bike or if he'd brought it with him but he had one.

And the others had sticks and things as well.

I couldn't see very clearly.

They were attacking Franz, three, four at a time, from different directions. They'd take two steps forwards quickly, and then retreat. Franz would whirl the tubing around in the downpour and when he'd sent off one lot, he'd turn to face the others.

But there were too many of them, even he couldn't manage.

With each fresh assault they were gaining ground, just a few centimetres, but they were getting closer all the time.

Someone do something! Dad, do something!

Dad ran towards the centre of the piazza, slipping on the stones in his sopping wet shoes.

"That's enough! That's enough! Stop it!"

But this time they weren't going to stop.

It was the final reckoning.

People were beginning to come, despite the rain.

They sheltered under the arcades. Who knows, maybe Mr Lulli was there too to enjoy the result of his words. Or maybe not: people like Mr Lulli don't come out in the open.

Show them, boys.

Oh, yes.

I wanted to run over to Johnny and shake him, say: Johnny, move!

Johnny would have known how to deal with the lot of them.

But I'm convinced Johnny wasn't really in the

piazza right then.

Johnny was Over There.

Max was a hair's breadth away from hitting Franz.

I discovered Magda next to me, her nails digging into my arm.

. . . That rumbling's getting louder all the time, and it's right above us . . .

Franz pushed Max back, turned again, lost his balance on the slimy stones and fell heavily to the ground like a wounded animal. The tubing slipped from his hand, we heard the clang of the metal distinctly as it bounced.

Help him, I thought, *help him*.

Franz got up again. He was enormous.

They were on him.

And then Franz screamed. A terrible never-ending scream.

The people from *Bar Grande* froze.

Max, breathing heavily, eyes shining with rage in the rain, froze too.

The black rain stopped instantly, just as it had begun.

Franz was screaming.

Then the sky – I swear – split open.

The slab of slate covering the village split in two.

Another sky appeared: this one was red.

The rumbling was so loud it seemed you could feel the houses vibrating.

"Planes," someone said.

I heard it very clearly, as if someone were speaking

into my ear.

"God in Heaven. They're aeroplanes."

Everyone has their own version of what happened next.

I found myself being hugged by Magda and Mum and Dad.

The sky – which maybe was ours or maybe not – was filled with red tracer bullet trails. The *rat tat tat tat* of anti-aircraft mingled with the huge, terrifying drone of the engines. It was everywhere, and I'm sure everyone was thinking the same thing: *I've got to get away.*

But there wasn't anywhere to run to.

People poured out into the streets, screaming.

Max let his chain drop without even noticing and fell like a stone to the ground. The others stopped in their tracks, as if paralysed.

Franz wasn't screaming any longer.

Johnny was still unmoving at his post.

Then the windows of the *Bar Grande* were blown out, showering the arcades with a hail of glass as people ran away. Next, the windows of the houses exploded along with all the TV screens, one by one – we heard the boom house by house – and as the wind raged, it dragged shreds of paper, plants and glass into the piazza. It made the alarms wail in the little villas with their garden gnomes and set the dogs howling.

Suddenly, the lights went out and in the darkness we could hear the drone of the planes as they moved away, slowly disappearing towards the horizon, until we couldn't hear them any longer, and we thought:

Don't let them come back.

They didn't come back.

It was silent. All you could hear was the rustling of sheets of newspaper blowing quietly about on the stones of the glass-strewn piazza.

By now the whole village was there, and they were all speechless.

Johnny gave a start and got up, walked without hurrying over to the old elm, took down his combat boots, put them on, knotted them carefully, and went and stood by Franz's side as if he were waiting for someone.

"There they are," said Magda. "They've been waiting for them for days."

We saw them arriving from the end of the Corso.

There were thousands of them.

Dressed in white, like ghosts in the dark.

They advanced slowly.

Boys and girls, small children, the odd adult.

The harvest of that sowing Over There.

They took an infinitely long time to file past, watched by the entire village.

Everyone – even those who didn't want to – was forced to *look at them*, so their faces and gestures were etched in people's minds.

They had to travel the whole length of the Corso – which is long – and cross the piazza – which is large – dragging themselves along with difficulty on rudimentary wooden crutches or leaning on improvised sticks.

They were holding one another up.

They passed by and we saw them disappear around the bend in the distance.

All that was left was the rustling of the pages of the *Gazzetta dello Sport* on the stones.

Johnny came up and hugged us.

"Let's go home," he said.

The sky was back to normal: limpid, clean, transparent.

There were even stars.

CHAPTER FOURTEEN

Johnny left the next day.

He put on jeans and a sweater again, filled a rucksack with a few things, dried out his field tent and rolled it up, packed up everything and went off at first light, like the sheriff does in classic westerns.

Franz helped him fix the carburettor on an old *Guzzi* bike which had been lying about the garage for years, then he borrowed some car or other and escorted him along the first stretch of road. The village was still deserted and covered with dust and bits of glass.

I watched Johnny leave with a heavy heart.

"Will he come back?" sobbed Magda.

"Yes, he'll be back. But I think you'd better find someone else."

"I'll never be able to!" she wailed.

Then life began again: the damage from that night was hurriedly repaired, there was a frantic rush to get a new TV. No trace remained of what had happened, at least, not one you could see.

I was sure everyone would talk about it, about what had happened, that they'd try to find a logical explanation, a reason, something. Instead, no one discussed it. If you brought it up, they changed the subject.

I don't know why.

Months passed and there were new things to talk about.

For example, I cut off my Mohican, took the pin out of my nose, stopped wearing dirty jumpers.

I don't know, I felt I no longer needed them. Or perhaps I was different.

Johnny sent us news from time to time: he sounded calm.

He didn't write many letters, but the ones he did were long and full of things and thoughts and places he'd visited. Every evening we'd all read them in the kitchen together.

One day, in the spring, Franz also disappeared. He went away without saying a word to anyone.

For a long time, I kept looking around for him whenever I crossed the piazza. I hoped I'd see him again, sitting there on a bench, with his shaven head and his studs and his grunts, busy crushing beer cans.

I didn't see him again.

One day a postcard arrived from a foreign country without any writing on it, not even a signature.

Well, Franz had always been a man of few words.

I often thought about him and Johnny travelling around the world. Perhaps one day they might meet up by chance in some place or other, maybe under a clean, clear and transparent sky, and they might listen to one of Janis' songs, share a beer and talk about whether they'd found any Answers.

Maybe they would. Maybe not.

But it isn't important to find answers.

The important thing is to look for them.

I often talk to Dad now, and he says that that's Freedom: to look for answers.

Maybe one day I'll go and look for my own, who knows?

Maybe here in the village people have improved since that November night. Maybe they've understood.

Maybe they've become a bit freer too.

Or maybe not.

This is a chapter of maybes.

Be patient.

How can you know anything for certain?

Conflict Prevention and Resolution Websites

www.brad.ac.uk/acad/confres

www.cartercentre.org

www.columbia.edu/cu/lweb/indiv/lehman/guides/icr.html

www.crinfo.org

www.crisisgroup.org

www.gmu.edu/departments/crdc

www.iimct.org

www.IMTD.org

www.jcr.sagepub.com

www.news.bbc.uk/cbbcnews/hi/teachers/citizenship

www.peacestudiesjournal.org.uk

www.policy.rutgers.edu/CNCR

www.SFCG.org

www.un.org

www.youthink.org

If you enjoyed reading *My Brother Johnny*, why not try...

Tina's Web by Alki Zei

Tina's life in Germany had been so happy, it never occurred to her that one day her parents might split. Or — worse still, send her back to Greece to live with her grandmother! But Tina doesn't mind anything any more. She's found the answer. With the help of a really amazing little blue pill... then lots more little pills... then lots of really incredible lies... Sometimes it's as if she's in heaven, sometimes she's crashing back down to earth, and now — there's no return. Or is there?

ISBN 97809551566-1-8

Coming Back by David Hill

Ryan has just got his licence. He's in the car with his mates. Tara likes to go running. She's on her way back home. Neither of them is paying much attention...

The accident that follows impacts many lives.

A moving and compelling story of recovery, told by one of New Zealand's foremost children s writers.

ISBN 09542330-2-6

Sobibor by Jean Molla

"I did it so they'd stop me," Emma said, when she was caught stealing biscuits from a supermarket. But Emma is hiding behind her tough words and her waif-like body...

Emma is sixteen and anorexic. Why does she do it? Is it her parents' indifference, the long family silences, the lies they tell each other? Emma wants to know the truth. She wants to understand the past.

When she discovers an old notebook in her grandparents' house, disturbing secrets emerge that demand an answer.

ISBN 09546912-4-5

Thistown by Malcolm McKay

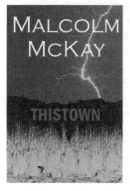

Somewhere beyond the rain, the wind and the stars, and as far from the Earth as it's possible to be, there was a town so old no one can remember how or when it began. It was a town where everyone remained exactly the same, a town where no one grew older, a town surrounded by a million miles of yellow corn which was so strange that if you went in you disappeared immediately. And perhaps the town would have stayed the same if they hadn't found the Sleeping Man. He changed everything. Forever.

ISBN 09546912-5-3

Blackmail by Thomas Feibel (Forthcoming)

Having tricked both his parents and his school, Johnny, 17, follows his rock idol on a national tour. But things don't go to plan when he has all his money stolen and the people around him end up dead — all because of an email he's mistakenly received from a criminal gang! Unaware that both the criminals and the police are after him, Johnny eventually tracks down his elusive rock idol and lives his dream...

ISBN 97809551566-2-5

Letters from Alain by Enrique Perez Diaz (Forthcoming)

Arturo, an 11 year old boy lives on the island of Cuba. One day, his best friend Alain goes away with his family on a small boat, in search of a better life in America. But the sea can be a perilous place... When Alain's dog returns mysteriously, the adults fear the worst. But Arturo begins to receive strange letters from his friend. What do they mean? And will his friend ever return?

The poignant tale of a child coming to terms with the realities of a troubled society.

ISBN 97809551566-4-9